"Here's the report," Tessa said, breaking in to his thoughts.

Ethan's hand brushed hers when he took the pages. A jolt raced through him, as if he had grabbed a live wire. His gaze flew to hers. Her eyes widened and a startled "oh" escaped her perfect mouth. The surprise in her eyes told him he wasn't alone in the reaction.

"Thanks again for your help with William and Kevin." Her eyes softened with gratitude, making Ethan's chest tighten.

"Be careful of Kevin. Despite the charming smile he so easily flashes, he's a con man. I can't guarantee he won't be violent, so if it comes to your life or the horse's, you're more valuable."

The expression in her eyes mellowed. "Thanks for the warning."

Would she thank him if she knew why he knew that truth about Kevin? His past mistakes wouldn't make a difference in their professional relationship, and apparently that was the only kind of relationship they'd have. Anything else would only lead to disaster.

Books by Leann Harris

Love Inspired

Second Chance Ranch
Redemption Ranch
Fresh-Start Ranch

Love Inspired Suspense

Hidden Deception
Guarded Secrets

LEANN HARRIS

When Leann Harris was first introduced to her husband in college she knew she would never date the man. He was a graduate student getting a PhD in physics, and Leann had purposely taken a second year of biology in high school to avoid taking physics. So much for first impressions. They have been married thirty-eight years and still approach life from very different angles.

After graduating from the University of Texas at Austin, Leann taught math and science to deaf high school students for a couple of years until the birth of her first child. When her youngest child started school, Leann decided to fulfill a lifelong dream, and she began writing.

She is a founding member and former president of the Dallas Area Romance Writers. Leann lives in Dallas, Texas, with her husband. Visit her at her website, www.leannharris.com.

Fresh-Start Ranch

Leann Harris

Love Inspired

Recycling programs
for this product may
not exist in your area.

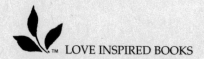 LOVE INSPIRED BOOKS

ISBN-13: 978-0-373-08255-1

FRESH-START RANCH

www.LoveInspiredBooks.com

Printed in U.S.A.

Blessed are all who take refuge in Him.
—*Psalms* 2:12

This is for my lovely daughter, Jennifer, whose prayers for her mother saw me through a dark time. You are exceptional.

Chapter One

Even though he'd only been gone for a few days, Ethan McClure sighed as he pulled into the drive leading to his family's ranch. But his relief turned to curiosity as he took in the old, beat-up brown pickup parked out front. He'd never seen that wreck before. Who did it belong to?

His mind still on the unknown truck, Ethan saw his dad hurrying from the barn. Ken McClure froze at the sight of his oldest son. "You're home."

Obviously. But the note of alarm in his father's voice put Ethan on edge. "What's wrong?" He climbed out of the truck, his luggage forgotten.

"Don't worry, son. Ranger's goin' to be fine. Tessa's got everything under control."

Ethan's stomach dropped. "Tessa?" He looked again at the beat-up truck, wondering what its owner had to do with his favorite horse. "Who's Tessa? And what's wrong with Ranger?"

Ranger whinnied, drawing Ethan's attention. Everything else forgotten, Ethan raced toward the barn, his tension zooming into high gear. It took a moment for his eyes to adjust to the dimness of the barn's interior.

"It's going to be okay, big guy," a woman crooned.

That didn't sound good. Down the rows of stalls, he saw Ranger. A small person was in the stall with him.

His father ran in behind him.

"Who's that?" Ethan demanded, not taking his eyes off Ranger.

"That's Doc's new partner, Dr. Tessa Grant."

Off balance, Ethan glanced at his father. "When did that happen?"

Ken swallowed. "She got here last week when you were in Boise."

Ethan knew that Doc Adams had finally made the decision to bring another vet into his practice, but Ethan hadn't realized it would happen *that* quickly. He'd been gone less than a week.

Ethan and Ken strode together toward Ranger's stall. His horse raised his head and nodded in greeting.

Ethan grabbed the bridle and rubbed Ranger's nose. "Hey, big guy." The woman stepped back from Ranger and met Ethan's gaze. Golden-brown curls framed her pixie face and her huge green eyes found a path straight into his heart.

Ethan jerked, though he wasn't sure if it was from his intense reaction to their eyes meeting or his surprise at the idea of this tiny woman as the new vet. Short and slim, if she didn't have a stethoscope around her neck, Ethan would've thought the woman standing beside his horse was a teenager, not a grown woman and certainly not someone who worked with large animals. "What's wrong with Ranger?" The tone of the question came out gruffer and harsher than Ethan expected. His father pointedly frowned at him.

The woman's brow shot up, and she stood up straight. "He's fine." Her tone made him think of the times his mother had scolded him for addressing her in a disrespectful tone when he tried to get out of chores. "He just got spooked by the weather last night. He has a few scrapes from flying debris, and I think he ran into the barbed-wire fence. He'll be fine."

Ethan looked at the wounds and nicks on Ranger's side.

"The storm last night just came up without any warning," his father explained. "A tornado touched down at the Barlows' ranch. They lost one storage shed. Several of our horses were out in the north pasture. First thing this morning I was able to get Ranger, Sadie and Ringo rounded up, and brought them in. Doc Adams and Dr. Grant have been out all day checking with the other ranchers, seeing to the different needs of the animals."

The woman shook her head. "That storm was something else. We had bad weather in Kentucky, but yesterday was—I felt like I was in a metal barrel with someone banging on it with a hammer." She held out her hand. "You must be the Ethan I've heard *so* much about. I'm Dr. Tessa Grant, Dr. Adams's new associate."

He felt as if he was in that same storm, disoriented and waiting for the next blow. "I am." His hand enveloped hers, but that small hand had a surprising number of calluses on it. "I did see some evidence of the storm as I drove in. Ringo and Sadie okay?"

"They've got a few cuts from flying debris, but they look fine." She patted Ranger's withers. "This guy took the worst of it."

Ethan bristled a little. He didn't know this person from Adam and no one touched his horse. "Maybe we should wait for Doc Adams."

"No need—I've this under control."

"He's kinda high-strung."

"I know." She went back to work, cleaning the last of the horse's wounds, but he thought he heard her mumble, "He's not the only one."

His father shifted. Ethan wasn't going to apologize for being concerned about his horse.

He also was having trouble wrapping his brain around the fact that the woman was a vet—a big-animal vet, no less. How could she do the job? She wasn't big enough or strong enough, as far as he was concerned. He turned to his father and opened his mouth, but his father's warning expression stopped him. But much to his embarrassment, he could only stare in amazement as Ranger stood docilely by while the lady vet finished working on him.

Ranger head-butted Ethan's hand, wanting attention. Ethan rubbed the big guy's nose. "Usually, Ranger's not so cooperative with exams," Ethan heard himself say. "He likes to give Dr. Adams a run for his money."

"You should've seen Tessa handle Ranger when she first got here," Ken eagerly explained. "She worked on Ringo, then Sadie before seeing to Ranger. He got jealous, and finally Ranger couldn't take the suspense anymore and turned to her."

"Really?" Amazed by his father's comment, Ethan knew his horse liked to be a pistol, dishing out a bad attitude. Doc and his dad had been on the wrong end of Ranger's mischief.

But he didn't like being ignored, either. Small or not, the vet must have some horse sense if she'd figured that out right from the start. Or had she gotten lucky?

"I wouldn't have believed it myself unless I saw it with my own eyes," Ken added.

The woman studied him. Ethan knew doubt showed on his face. The telltale tightening of her right hand told him he wasn't the first to question her skill.

"When I was growing up," Tessa explained, addressing Ken, "the stable manager I worked with was a genius with horses—that 'horse whisperer' kind of thing. He was truly amazing. He taught me how to get acquainted with horses. I haven't found a single horse who's given me grief." She glanced over her shoulder. "A lot of owners, but not the horses."

Ethan didn't doubt that other owners had trouble with her. He wondered if she had the strength to help with a distressed pregnancy, a breech foal or an angry cow that was on a rampage. Could she wrestle a branch out of a cow's throat like Dr. Adams did a couple of years ago?

"You need anything else, Dr. Grant?" Ken asked.

"I don't think so. I'll leave some salve for the horses and drop by next week to see how things are progressing."

Ken nodded. "You coming, son?"

"I'll just stay here and help Dr. Grant with Ranger."

Ken laughed and walked out of the barn.

Ethan watched carefully as Dr. Grant finished with Ranger. She had a way with his mount as if she had some connection to him. She gave Ranger plenty of affection, murmuring sweet words and pats. His horse ate it up as if no one had ever praised him. Those sweet words charmed more than his horse—Ethan felt himself respond to that affectionate tone, too. It'd been so long since that bright morning, standing in the church, waiting for his bride that never showed.

He mentally jerked himself out of the painful memory. "So what made you come out here to New Mexico?"

"I graduated from Purdue, same as Dr. Adams. I got the call from him about six weeks ago. He asked if I wanted to practice in a rural setting and pass up the glamour of an urban practice. He said he needed a young associate."

Her story made sense. Ethan and his dad had noticed that Dr. Adams wasn't moving quite as fast as he used to. A couple of months ago, one of their cows had kicked out and Doc hadn't moved quick enough to avoid that hoof. Doc had to spend a few hours at the house, an ice pack wrapped around his leg.

"I laughed and told him I'd love to practice out here, but did he realize my size. He said that he knew, but asked if I was willing to give it a try. I jumped at the chance," she added, turning to put away her things. "I wasn't interested in working in a practice that only dealt with dogs, cats and assorted pets." She pulled her stethoscope off her neck and put it in what looked like a tackle box.

He waited for the rest of her answer. "Why not?"

"My love is horses. I grew up in Kentucky and we had a full stable." Her wistful smile told him she was recalling good memories. "I loved working with them. Hasn't anyone told you that horses have a special place in little girls' hearts? I knew early on that I wanted to be a vet and work with horses. I had a lot of my professors and other people try to talk me out of it, but sometimes you just know what God wants you to do."

He eyed her size. When his gaze met hers, he saw the determination glowing there. Before he could say anything or stick his foot into his mouth again, his cell phone rang, saving him from having to eat shoe leather again.

Saved by Mountain Bell before he uttered *the* comment she hated: *Aren't you too short? And a girl?*

Tessa ran into that attitude far too often, first from her mother and close friends, then from the other students in vet school. She learned quickly to respond to their doubts with a smile, a joke, but knew she had to work twice as hard as her male counterparts to prove herself. So why did doubt from this tall—over six feet—handsome man with chestnut-color hair and piercing gray eyes jab her in the heart? She knew how to deflect those comments, so why had she mumbled that crack about Ranger's owner?

She knew God had called her to be a vet, given her the talent. Despite the odds against her, God had been with her through the lean times after her father deserted the family and they'd lost the family horse farm because of his gambling debts. God had been there with her in school, helping her through the nasty and despicable comments and opposition she faced from professors and fellow students. And He'd been there when she'd learned her fiancé wanted to marry her as his ticket through law school. She survived it all, so why'd this tall rancher suddenly get to her?

Her wounded heart needed to stay behind the walls she'd built and not be tempted by a good-looking cowboy.

"You believe in me," she whispered to Ranger, stroking his neck. The horse turned his head as if agreeing with her.

Her phone rang. She pulled it out of the pocket of her jeans and flipped it open. "Dr. Grant."

"Tessa, this is Dr. Adams. The local horse rescue group is seizing some horses this afternoon. I can't get there since I'm scheduled for surgery in a few minutes. Since you've worked with rescue groups before, I want you to go out to the Moores' ranch where the seizure will occur and oversee it."

"Okay, but I don't know where that ranch is located." She glanced at Ethan.

"Is Ethan there at the ranch?"

"Yes."

"He's the head of the local rescue group. The group's lawyer is calling him now. He can show you."

She looked at him. "Okay, I'll follow him." Hanging up, she waited for Ethan to finish his call. When he did, he turned to her.

"I need to go."

"I know. Dr. Adams just called and wants me to help with the seizure and document it. Since I am not familiar with this area, I'll need to follow you out to the Moore ranch."

"You've worked with a rescue group before?" His tone made it clear he still doubted her skill.

"Yes. In high school I worked summers with the local vet. We went on several rescues. I kept active in the organization through college and then in veterinary training. I've done rescues in Kentucky, Ohio, Montana and Wyoming."

"Good, because we're going to put your expertise to work. We've got twenty horses that need our help." He studied her.

If he thought the size of the rescue would worry her, he thought wrong. "Lead the way," she answered, without a moment of hesitation.

He studied her for a moment before coming to some decision. There he nodded, turned and walked out of the barn. Tessa hurried to put the last of her equipment in her medical bag and raced out after him. Ethan had already pulled his truck out of the driveway. A moment of panic shot through her. Was he going to leave without her? She hurried to his truck. The driver-side window was down. He stopped by her.

"I'm going to drive around the barn and hook up the trailer."

"You need help?"

He gave her an odd look. "I'll do it. Just be ready to leave when I drive by."

"You've got it."

She raced to her trusty, dented, secondhand F-150 truck, put her bag in the bed and hopped into the cab. She started the ignition and turned the truck around and waited, frowning a little at the noise the engine was making. Her baby, although eighteen years old, hadn't failed her yet, but its time was coming. She couldn't keep duct-taping the seats and hoses much longer.

Ethan's truck rumbled by, turning her thoughts to the drive ahead. She still wasn't as familiar with the roads around this part of New Mexico as she'd like. It didn't help that a lot of the ranches she visited were off small easy-to-miss roads. Doc had given her an old dog-eared map of the area, telling her to use it because it showed all the roads in the area which might not show up on any modern device.

She'd doubted Doc's warning and accidentally left the map at the office yesterday. Once she discovered that, she'd told herself that her modern technology was better. The

GPS device had been a graduation gift from her mother. But Tessa learned quickly the spotty reception in the canyons in this rural area made the new technology undependable. The device failed her completely, leaving her driving around the area for close to two hours, until she pulled into a ranch and asked directions. The couple, the Cousinses, smiled, commiserated then gave her directions. She wouldn't repeat the mistake a second time.

After twenty-five minutes, Ethan's truck turned off the road onto a private drive. There were six other pickups with trailers parked around the interior gate. The ranch house showed signs of neglect, as did the stables. One man, who seemed to have come from the house, yelled at the others to go away, a shotgun cradled in his left arm.

"If you don't leave, I'm going to start shooting," the man shouted.

A handsome woman in a business suit and high heels stepped forward and waved a piece of paper in the air. "William, we have a court order to seize the horses."

"I don't care what you've got. You make one move to take my horses, you'll be sorry."

The woman turned around and saw Ethan. She strode to his side. "Got any ideas?"

He stiffened. "Have you called Joe?"

"Of course. I called the sheriff's office before we left," she snapped. "Joe should be here any minute. We wouldn't have approached William, but he came charging out of the house like a mad bull."

The expression on William's face hadn't changed. He wanted a fight. "Let's wait," Ethan muttered.

"Where are the horses?" Tessa asked, coming to their sides.

The woman looked at her.

"I'm Dr. Adams's new associate." Tessa introduced herself, answering the question on the woman's face. "Dr. Grant."

"Mary Jensen, the lawyer for this local rescue group." She offered her hand to Tessa. Turning, she looked back at the dilapidated stables. "Some of the horses are in the stables, and there's a paddock in back of the house where the rest are kept."

They heard a distressed whinny come from inside the miserable excuse for a stable. The man, William, glanced over his shoulder, then looked back at the group. Clearly, he was torn whether to go to the animal or hold off the group.

Tessa moved toward the man. "I'm a vet. Dr. Grant. Can I offer you any assistance?" Tessa knew a cry of pain when she heard one. Was the man more concerned for his animals than the people trying to take them away? With his confusion clearly etched on his face, he looked back at the stables, then at her.

The horse whinnied again.

The man's face lost all color, and he looked back at the stables.

Something was wrong. Terribly wrong.

The moments stretched out as they all stood silent, waiting, waiting for his decision. Tessa prayed.

"Yeah, my mare needs some help," William said at last. "She's been down too long and the foal ain't coming."

"Would you let me help?"

He looked around the group, his jaw tense. "Only you."

"That's fine." She looked back at Ethan. "Will you bring my medical kit?"

"Sure." He walked back to her truck.

The man opened the gate and motioned her in. Closing it behind her, he walked her into the stable. He rested the shotgun by the open door.

"My mare's in the last stall on the left."

Tessa hurried to the stall. The white horse was on her side on a pile of hay, her eyes rolled back in her head. The hay wasn't clean and the mare was seriously underweight.

"Hello, girl. I'm here to help you," Tessa crooned. "Will you let me?" Tessa stepped to the mare's side. The horse didn't raise her head. "What's her name?"

"Lady."

Gingerly, Tessa knelt by the mare's bloated side. She ran her palms over the horse's flank to see if she could feel the position of the foal.

A hard knot was there right above the horse's back hip. "Okay, momma, I'm going to see if

I can feel your baby's feet." Tessa turned to the owner. "How long has she been down?"

"Don't know." He shrugged. "When I walked in this morning to check on her, she was like that."

"I need my medical bag."

The man disappeared for a moment, then reappeared with her tackle-box medical kit. She threw open the lid and poured the cleanser over her hands. "Okay, Lady, let's see how your baby's doing."

Tessa tried to find the foal's hooves, but instead found the tail. She sat back on her heels and looked up at the owner. "The foal's breech."

The man lost his color. "I don't want to lose that baby. She's sold."

Tessa tried to get her mind around what she'd just heard.

"I need for you to save that foal."

Lord, give me grace. It sounded as if the man was more concerned with his money than the horse. "I'm going to try to turn the foal, but—" Nothing else needed to be said.

"William, this is Sheriff Teague," came the

voice over a bullhorn. "I'm here to enforce the court order."

The owner disappeared. Tessa didn't pay attention to the conversation outside. She looked at the mare and prayed.

Ethan watched as William came out of the stables. He held the shotgun in his right hand.

"Put that thing down, William, before you hurt yourself," Sheriff Joe Teague ordered.

William looked at the people standing around. "This isn't right. You shouldn't be taking Ma's horses."

"You can take that up with the judge."

Ethan carefully watched William. He had been in Ethan's sister's graduating class. As a teenager, William hadn't really fit in with either the kids in the rodeo circuit or the kids who were on the college track. He'd been a loner and apparently still didn't know his calling.

They heard another whinny followed by Tessa's voice. "Easy, girl."

William turned and started toward the stable. "You better hurry before my mother gets back, because she'll object." He disappeared into the stables.

The sheriff turned to the gathered crowd. "No sense in moving that mare until she's delivered. Let's get the rest of these animals loaded."

Ethan knew exactly where he needed to go. He walked into the stables and saw William standing at the last stall at the back of the structure. When he looked at Ethan, William's ashen face sent alarm bells going off in Ethan's head.

He rushed to the stall and saw Tessa on her knees. Sweat plastered the curls to her face and neck. Her eyes met his. He saw her concern and seriousness of the situation, but he also saw a woman who knew what needed to be done.

"Can I help?"

"The foal is breech and I need to turn it."

"What do you need for me to do?"

"Talk to this sweet lady and calm her while I work to turn the foal."

Could she do it? He didn't know, but they were about to find out.

As they worked together, they were able to rotate the foal so the front legs were in the right position. Ethan helped Tessa, keeping the mare calm.

"That's it, Lady. You're doing a great job." Tessa looked at Ethan. "One of the foal's legs is still folded partially under the body. I'm going to try to straighten it out."

The mare looked at Tessa, her liquid brown eyes focused on the doctor.

"I'm trying, girl." Tessa didn't panic but worked at trying to straighten out the one leg. Tessa reached it and grabbed the second hoof and pulled it forward. Lady gave a sigh.

In the next instant, both legs and a head appeared. Lady took over from there, and gave the final push.

Tessa sat back on her heels and smiled. "We—" she looked at him, then Lady "—did it."

Chapter Two

Tessa settled the blanket around the filly's shivering form. The miracle of birth always brought tears to her eyes. No matter how many births she attended, they were always awe inspiring. Ethan steadied the mare as she struggled to her feet.

Tessa's eyes met his. Satisfaction glowed there.

"Thanks for the help," she murmured. Oddly, they had worked well together, anticipating each other during Hope's birth.

William's voice floated into the stables. "Ma, they have a court order."

"I don't care," came the shrill reply. "They

don't have the right. I've sold that foal and ain't goin' to give back the money."

Tessa met Ethan's gaze. His lips pressed into a line of disgust.

The sheriff appeared in the doorway. "If you're ready, I'd like to get out of here ASAP."

"We're ready," Tessa answered.

"I'll carry the foal," Ethan told them, "and that should take care of the mare. She'll follow."

"Put a bridle on her," Tessa instructed as she cleaned up. "It will help later."

"So you plan on taking the horses to the vet's place?" Sheriff Teague asked.

The clinic couldn't handle all the horses long-term, but there might be another place the rescue group used. For now it would be easier to assess the horses' state of health at the clinic. She could also document their condition and take pictures, which she hadn't been able to do because of the emergency. "Is there another facility the rescue group uses?" Tessa asked.

"No." Ethan looked around for a bridle. When he didn't spot one, he found a piece of rope and fashioned it into a halter to go over the mare's head. "The last time we did a rescue, Doc kept the horses at his clinic, but then there were only twelve horses. The next day we found foster homes for the animals."

Ethan walked to Tessa's side and scooped up the foal. The filly wouldn't make it onto the trailer on such shaky legs.

"I'll grab my medical bag and Momma's lead."

Ethan waited until Tessa had gathered her tackle box before he walked outside. On unsteady legs, the mother horse followed her baby. Tessa caught the trailing end of the rope as a precaution.

Out in the yard, an elderly woman lunged at Ethan. Sheriff Teague stepped in her way.

"He can't take the foal," the woman argued. "She's spoken for."

Ethan walked into his trailer and set the foal on her feet. The foal stumbled around, trying to catch her balance. The mare followed. Ethan tied her to the inside O-ring, anchoring the rope.

"Stop him," the woman yelled.

"Take it up with the judge, Doris," the sheriff replied.

She came face-to-face with Ethan. "You take care of that foal."

Tessa stared in amazement at the woman. She hadn't taken care of the mother horse and now was worried about the foal? Something wasn't right.

"The doc will take good care of her," Ethan answered, but his tone, understanding yet firm, surprised Tessa.

The woman shook her finger at Ethan. "You be sure."

"What you need to worry about, Doris, is calling the county court and seeing when your hearing is scheduled. You can complain to the judge," the sheriff interjected.

Doris snarled at him.

Ethan turned his back on the woman and walked Tessa to the cab of her truck. Tessa wondered if the woman might rush them.

"Don't worry," Ethan whispered. "Doris talks big, but she won't do anything outright in front of everyone."

"How do you know?"

"I've known her all my life."

Tessa was pretty sure she knew what that meant—Doris would have someone else do her dirty work. "I'll see you back at Doc's office." He turned, starting toward his truck. He paused, turned and gave her a thumbs-up. "You did a great job delivering that foal, Doc."

The praise shocked Tessa. He didn't wait for a response, just headed toward her truck.

But as they drove back to the clinic, she thought about Ethan's words. She wasn't the only one who'd done well. It'd been touch-and-go there. As they worked to save the foal, he'd accurately anticipated her needs before she voiced them.

They made a good working team.

The thought shook her to her core and set her protective instincts on alert.

Ethan walked down the center aisle of the hospital barn, looking for Tessa. He carried a cup of hot, fresh coffee. He would relieve Tessa and take the next shift of watching and hand-feeding Momma and her babe. It was close to four in the morning. Once they'd gotten back to the veterinary hospital, Tessa and Dr. Adams had worked evaluating the horses, starting IVs and seeing to the needs of the most critical of the animals. They documented their work so it could be used in court. Not once had Doc Adams had to direct Tessa. She knew her stuff. One of the other volunteers had commented that Doc's new partner knew her way around a horse. Word would quickly spread about her abilities.

After initial evaluations, she checked each horse a second time, then took the second shift of feeding Lady, the foal's dam. They'd sent all the other volunteers home after the horses were settled outside in the paddock.

Doc had taken the first shift of watching mare and foal. Now it was Ethan's turn to take the shift from four to seven. He stopped at the door to the stall. Tessa sat on a three-legged stool beside the sling of hay attached to the sidewall of the stall.

Tessa's eyes were closed. But despite her tired, vulnerable appearance, he knew his perspective on her had undergone a major change. After what they'd been through yesterday, looking at Tessa now, she didn't look like a high school freshman he first mistook her for. Instead, what he saw was a petite woman who had a dazzling smile and a voice that could calm the most nervous horse or stressed person. He also saw a determined soul. The lady knew her stuff. But what he felt went deeper than appreciation for her skill.

He hadn't been prepared for his pull to her, after he got over the initial shock of finding her tending his mount. He was gun-shy about commitments after his disastrous engagement to Mary.

Of course, it didn't help that Mary had suddenly reappeared in his life a month ago as the replacement lawyer for the rescue group, poking at the old wound. Over the years, while he'd seen her in passing, since her parents owned the ranch next to his family's ranch, he hadn't had to talk to her. But in the weeks she'd been here, dealing with her had opened up old hurts, shame and embarrassment. He was way too raw to consider romance again.

A delicate snore drew his attention back to Tessa.

The mare woke and started to nibble the hay and caught several strands of Tessa's hair. Tessa woke with a jerk. The horse lipped another few stalks of hay. Tessa reached up and rubbed the horse's nose. "That's right, Momma, eat the hay, not the vet's hair. We want a healthy momma and baby, not a bald vet." Turning her head, Tessa noticed him. "Is that coffee for me?"

"It is. I've already finished my cup and thought you might need some fortification."

"A man after my own heart." The instant the last word fell from her lips, her eyes widened and her cheeks turned pink. The words made him feel a little awkward, too, but he couldn't help but smile when she looked so cute.

"Huh, I mean—"

Shaking his head, he said, "I know what you meant." He handed her the mug. Cradling it between her hands, she sipped the brew.

"That's so good." She took another sip. "Thanks."

He didn't think anything about his actions. It was simply a gesture he would've made for anyone who'd worked as hard as she had, but he doubted he would've felt the same happiness at her thanks if the person doing the thanking was Ollie, the old grizzled foreman at his brother's therapy ranch. What was going on with him?

"How's this girl doing?" he asked as he fed the mare another handful of hay, eager to change the subject.

"So-so but steady." Tessa stood and checked the bag of fluid. "I need to get another one of these." Setting down her cup on the stool, she disappeared around the door of the stall.

She soon returned to the entrance to the stall with a new IV bag. She quickly changed out the bag. Another yawn seized her.

"Why don't you grab a couple hours of shut-eye? I'll watch these two."

"Not that I don't appreciate the help, but don't you need to get back home?"

"I talked with my folks around midnight, updating them on the rescue. I told them I'd probably spend the night here, helping. It's not the first time Doc and I have been babysitting sick, rescued animals."

She studied him, and he knew she was evaluating him. Apparently, he passed the test because she nodded. "Thanks." She disappeared down the aisle.

The foal made her way to her momma and began to nurse. Ethan had to smile at the new life that Tessa and he had a hand in. They worked well together.

And that made him antsy. He didn't want to let another woman into his life. Not yet, maybe not ever again.

A few hours later, Dr. Adams appeared in the stall opening. "You ready to eat some breakfast?"

Ethan looked at the sleeping foal. She seemed stronger, but still favored her right front leg. "I am. The horses seem to be doing well."

"Good. The rest of the horses are faring well, too. Come on into the kitchen and have some breakfast. I've got a feeling that it's going to get busy sooner than we want. Other ranchers will be coming today to get horses to house."

With a final glance, Ethan stood and stretched. He joined Doc outside the stall and closed the door behind him. As they walked through the screened-in breezeway that ran from the barn past the operating room and offices to the house, Ethan nailed Doc with a look. "Imagine my surprise yesterday, when I walked into my barn and found this unknown person handling Ranger."

A mischievous smile crossed Doc's face. "That so?"

"Yup."

"Your dad knew Tessa and I had divided up the calls after the storm," the older man offered innocently. "Your folks were here right after Tessa arrived. Your mom fixed up the spare room for her. Besides, you knew I'd hired a new vet."

Doc scored a point. "True. I remember you saying you hired a Dr. T. Grant who graduated from Purdue. No one mentioned the *T* stood for Tessa, not Tony or Terry, nor did you mention when Dr. Grant would get here."

"Does it matter, Ethan?"

Ethan blushed. "No, but—"

Doc opened the door to the kitchen. "But what?"

"I wasn't expecting a girl," he sputtered, feeling supremely stupid.

"Catch up with the times, son. Tessa graduated in the top 10 percent of her class, and when I learned she grew up on a horse farm in Kentucky, I knew we'd be lucky to have her. I just prayed that she'd be willing to come out here. New Mexico is beautiful but in a different way from Kentucky. If this land doesn't call to your heart, then you won't be happy."

Ethan grabbed a mug from the cabinet and poured himself some coffee. What Doc said was true. If you didn't feel easy with this rugged land, then you wouldn't be happy, as evidenced by the vet who came for six months to sub for Doc when he went home to see his family. When Doc returned to the clinic, he asked the young vet if he wanted to stay and join Doc's practice. He politely declined and went back to Wisconsin. Doc tried a couple of other times, but to no avail. If Tessa truly did settle in, Ethan knew it would be a load off Doc's mind. But was Tessa really the right choice for their community?

"Put some bread in the toaster," Doc ordered

from his position by the stove. There were eggs in a skillet and bacon on a plate next to him.

Ethan knew this kitchen as well as he knew the kitchen at home. He'd spent many an hour in here with Doc talking. "Since you came from that part of the country, weren't you worried about her coming?"

Doc served up the eggs. He made three plates and brought two of them to the table. After placing several strips of bacon on the third plate, he brought the rest to the table. "I gave it a fifty-fifty chance. Horse country in Kentucky is some of the most beautiful I've seen."

"So why'd you come out to New Mexico?" Ethan asked. Up to this moment, it had never occurred to him to ask.

His eyes took on a faraway look. Ethan thought Doc might not answer him. Ethan had shared with this man the darkest secrets of his life, and Doc had not betrayed that confidence. But as Ethan thought about it, Doc had shared sparingly about his life before he came here.

Finally, Doc said, "I needed a new beginning."

The answer shocked Ethan. He wanted to ask more, but looking at the older man, Ethan knew not to push.

Doc dug into his eggs. "This land has a beauty that I've come to love, and I hope Tessa will come to love it, too."

As they quietly ate, Ethan's mind filled with questions about Doc's past.

"I was glad to have Tessa yesterday," Doc said, picking up his coffee. "She proved herself with the storm, then with that rescue. Do you think I could've done better with that foal?"

Ethan thought about it. Could Doc have done better? "Hard to say. You might've been able to position that foal better."

Doc nodded. "I know."

"You know what?" Tessa asked from the doorway. Her voice rang clear and strong.

Ethan shoved the last of the eggs in his mouth. Let Doc handle that response.

She sniffed the air. "Is that coffee I smell?"

"Yup," Doc answered. "And eggs and bacon."

She quickly stepped into the room. Dressed in a pair of jeans, boots and a white long-sleeved shirt, she nearly knocked Ethan's socks off. "Good," she said, "because I wasn't up for cooking anything this morning, but smelling the coffee and bacon, my stomach told me it's time to eat." After filling a mug, she threw a piece of bread in the toaster and brought her plate to the table. "So what do you know?" She looked from Doc to Ethan.

"Ethan was just saying you knew exactly what to do to care for those rescued horses yesterday. And you did a great job with the birth."

Her fork stopped halfway to her mouth. Her gaze moved from Doc to Ethan. She placed the food in her mouth and nodded.

"Ethan says he thinks you did a nice job delivering the foal."

Tessa turned to Ethan, surprise in her eyes. He saw what his faith in her meant and felt ashamed that he hadn't actually said any of those things.

"It was a team effort." Tessa buttered her toast. "We need to watch Hope's leg. She wasn't too sure standing on it last night. The strain of the birth might've damaged that ligament in her foreleg."

Cupping his coffee in both hands, Ethan said, "I didn't notice much of a limp when the foal started nursing this last time. I might've been a little sleepy, but things might already be working out."

"Good."

The phone rang. "The day begins," Doc muttered as he stood and answered the phone. "Hello. Yes, Mary, we've done the initial evaluation of the horses. All of them made it through the night." Doc looked from Tessa to Ethan. "You need the report that soon?" He frowned. "Okay. Drop by tonight and we'll have the report. Also, I'll have a list of where each of the horses will be housed." After saying goodbye, he hung up.

"Mary wants a written report on the condition of each horse. She'll print out the pictures she took so we can petition the judge for custody." Doc sat down beside Tessa. "Have you written any reports for court fights?"

"Yes."

"Good, because I'm all thumbs and can't type worth spit. Can you have a report for Mary by five today?"

"Low man on the totem pole, huh?" A grin followed the question.

Doc threw his head back and laughed. Tessa smiled.

"You nailed it."

As Ethan looked from one vet to another, he had the oddest feeling of hearing an echo. There was a similarity. He shrugged it off, telling himself he was just tired.

The sound of tires squealing to a stop followed by the slamming of car doors stopped the jocularity.

Instantly, Ethan and Doc were on their feet, heading for the door.

"Grab the cordless phone," Ethan shot over his shoulder, his stomach tight, "and be prepared to call the sheriff." Ethan followed Doc outside.

"What's wrong?" Tessa asked.

"No rancher would've come to as reckless a stop in front of the animal hospital. It's trouble."

It turned out to be William Moore and his

mother. William held a rifle and his mother looked as if she was spoiling for a fight.

He'd been right—they sure looked like trouble.

Chapter Three

Tessa didn't wait for Ethan to tell her to call. She dialed 911 and told the dispatcher what the problem was while keeping an ear out for the conversation outside.

"Mornin', Doris," Doc called out, his voice congenial.

"It will be when I get my horses," she snapped.

Doc walked toward her. "You'll be happy to know all the horses made it through the night. It was tough going, though, getting your mare and her foal through those hours. We took turns hand-feeding them."

Doris glared at him. "I didn't need your help. My mare would've done just fine. It was all that commotion that your team stirred up that gave her trouble."

Just how much in denial was this woman? It wasn't unusual for people who neglected animals not to see what they'd done, but Doris brought it to a whole new level.

"William, go get the horses," Doris commanded.

William's eyes widened. "But Ma—"

"Don't Ma me. Get the horses."

Tessa scrambled outside into the parking lot. "If you move either of those horses, you might kill them."

Doris's attention focused on Tessa. "What are you talking about?"

"The mare might not make it back to your stable. And the foal, her leg was in the wrong position when she was born. She has a slight limp. If they're left here, we can oversee their medical condition and help at this critical junction. It's their best chance to survive and fully recover."

For the first time, the hostility in Doris's expression softened.

"She's got a point, Ma."

"Dr. Grant is right in her assessment, Doris," the older veterinarian confirmed. "The best choice for your animals is to leave them here. Do you want to see how they're doing?"

Doris put her hands on her hips and glared. "Of course."

"Come in and see for yourself." Doc motioned Doris into the breezeway.

Ethan stepped to William's side. "Why don't you put that rifle down before someone gets hurt?"

Relief swept across the young man's face. "Ma thought we needed the show of strength." He looked at his mother. She nodded and he put the rifle on the floor behind the seats in the cab.

William moved behind his mother with Ethan and Tessa trailing behind.

Doc walked down the breezeway to the barn. "This way, Doris."

She shook her finger at Doc. "Okay, but I'm not giving up on getting my horses back."

"I'd expect nothing less," he answered.

Doris and William walked through the barn door.

"You handled that well," Ethan whispered to Tessa.

"You're surprised?"

"Nope."

Tessa didn't know how to take his answer. He didn't wait for her but caught up with William. Tessa followed after, trying to decide how she felt about Ethan McClure.

The man seemed to be a bag of walking contradictions. He went from skepticism to approval. He questioned her qualifications yet took directions well from her last night, didn't hesitate and did his turn nursing the horses without complaint. His skills were excellent, but that didn't surprise her, his being a rancher. Had he changed his mind about her or would he at some point call her ability into question again?

She couldn't get a good read on him and that made her jumpy.

Doris stopped and looked into the stall. Lady nibbled the feed, while her foal rested on a pile of clean hay in the corner of the stall.

"They're looking fine to me," Doris commented.

Tessa joined them by the stall door. She prayed for the right words. "That's because we stayed with them all night. Lady's had two IVs." Doc must've removed the IV from the mare. "We can treat them medically. Since Dr. Adams and I are here, we can oversee any complications. We've got fluids, antibiotics and high-grade feed for them. That foal needs some TLC for her leg. No one is going to want a horse that can't be ridden."

Doris wavered.

"And you'll have your time in court to argue for getting them back," Ethan added. "It would be to your advantage to cooperate with us, Doris. I'll be sure to tell the judge you did."

The older woman's eyes narrowed, but she nodded grudgingly. "All right, but you be sure to do that."

"I will."

They walked outside and discovered Sheriff Teague there.

"Everything okay out here?" Joe asked, getting out of his patrol unit.

Doris frowned, but she didn't respond.

"Everything's fine," Doc Adams answered. He turned to Doris.

She didn't comment, just glared at them, then climbed into the truck, slamming the passenger-side door. William got into the driver's seat and they sped off, leaving a cloud of dust.

As Tessa watched the truck disappear, she knew deep in her gut this wasn't going to be the last time she'd have a run-in with Doris and her son. She just hoped that Doc—and Ethan—would be there to calm things down when trouble came knocking again.

Tessa sat in the clinic office the next day, staring at the report she'd just finished. She clicked the print button. Too many times she'd had to write similar reports. Doc had called Mary back and told her the report would take another day, due to the increased workload at the clinic that had them scrambling. Tessa could easily see why Doc Adams needed another vet to help.

Standing, she walked to the printer. Each time she participated in a rescue and saw how people neglected their horses, her heart broke.

But God had given her this eternal hope that no matter how bleak, He could shine a light into any darkness, as witnessed by Hope's birth.

She heard a car engine outside, then car doors slam.

As she gathered the pages from the printer, she heard the screen door creak open. She strode out of the office into the waiting area. Looking through the window, she saw a horse trailer.

Unease crept up her spine. Doc had left for one of the ranches north of the clinic about forty-five minutes ago.

Scout, the clinic's dog, started barking, followed by the sound of another distressed whinny. Tessa raced into the barn. William and another man stood by Lady and Hope's stall.

"What are you doing?" Tessa demanded in her best command voice.

The men whirled. "Who are you?" the stranger asked.

"I'm Dr. Grant, one of the vets here."

The man's mouth curved into an oh-you're-a-girl-and-I-can-charm-you smile. "You're too cute and young to be a vet. Why, you can't be more than sixteen."

His grating attitude left her cold.

William jumped in. "No, she's the vet who delivered the foal. I saw it with my own eyes."

The other man's brow rose. "Ah, beautiful and skilled."

She wasn't buying his line. "What are you doing here, William? I thought we'd resolved this issue yesterday with you and your mother."

"Aw, don't call Willy that. He's a good ol' boy and not the stuffed shirt his old man was," the stranger interrupted.

Tessa stepped past Mr. Charm into the stall. "What are you doing, William?" she asked again. William glanced over her shoulder at the stranger.

"Willy wanted me to see my investment," the man offered, his voice coming from behind her.

Tessa turned to face the stranger. She stood by William's side. "I'm sure William told you that you'll have to take that up with the court."

He shrugged and took a menacing step toward her. "I've already paid for the foal."

William shifted his weight from one foot to another. Tessa noticed the panicked look on his face. She squared her shoulders and put authority into her words. "I'm sure the court will take that into account."

The stranger's fake smile melted and his eyes went cold. "Why bother the courts?"

Tessa understood perfectly that the stranger was trying to intimidate her. She opened her mouth to respond, but another voice cut in.

"Because, Kevin, the sheriff's already seized the animals. And if you're trying to take the foal, you'll be breaking the law, subject to arrest and then they'll have an access into all sorts of information about you."

The man whirled to face Ethan. Tessa had never seen a better sight than the tall rancher. She breathed a prayer of thanks.

"Ah, Ethan McClure, the hero of Cibola High School's football team, coming to the little lady's rescue," the stranger sneered.

Tessa's eyes narrowed, ready to correct the situation, but Ethan spoke first.

"If you've got a bone to pick, take it up with the judge. But be warned, Kevin, you need to bring your lawyer, because Mary will be there representing the rescue group, pressing our case."

"Mary Jensen? You mean the little lady who left you standing at the altar? That Mary Jensen?" Kevin ended his taunt with a satisfied grin.

The comment rocked Tessa back on her heels. Ethan didn't flinch, but Tessa noticed his hand clenched as if he was holding back his anger. "My history doesn't change the facts. You're not taking that foal anywhere."

Kevin's smirk turned into a glare. "We'll see about that." He looked at William and nodded to him to leave. As Kevin walked by Ethan, he stopped. "You're not quite as righteous as folks think, hey, buddy? I know our hero has feet of clay."

Ethan didn't respond, but held his ground.

Kevin laughed. "I'll see ya." He winked at Tessa and walked out of the stables.

The tension holding her upright eased, and she took a deep breath. The shock of Kevin's words still reverberated through her. Mary and Ethan had been engaged?

"You okay?" Ethan asked, coming to her side.

She gave a shaky laugh. "Yeah, but William's determination to get Hope just seems—oh, I don't know—so intense…desperate." She thought about the things that Kevin threw at Ethan. What was going on? It was none of her business, she reminded herself. She had to stay focused on the horse.

"That bothers me, too." Ethan rubbed the back of his neck. "There's something there that doesn't seem right. It's like when my sister decided to wear one of my belts and put it back in the closet in my room, but she put it in the wrong place. It took me a day to understand what was bothering me."

Tessa's eyes went wide with surprise. "Are you kidding me?"

"No, I think William's up to something."

"I wasn't talking about that. You knew when your sister borrowed your belt?" Kevin had thrown some pretty heavy accusations at Ethan and he was talking about his sister wearing his belt?

His eyes cut to hers, and his mouth twitched, disarming the tension. "She was bad about borrowing things. I'd walk into the kitchen and find her wearing one of my shirts or sweat-shirts or belts. Or my brother's stuff." The way his brows knitted into a frown made her want to laugh.

"Wow." Talk about ignoring the issue. She thought about calling him on it but she didn't feel it was right to push.

"My example was to point out when some-thing feels wrong."

"I see." She agreed with that, as far as it went.

He shrugged. "The foal seems to be walk-ing without a limp," he commented, changing the subject.

Her mind snapped back to the present. "That's what I hoped would happen. She's also nursing well." Tessa ran her hands down the mare's side. "Momma's also doing well. The IV fluids helped.

"This lady has a will to live. Babies will do

that to a mother." When she looked up, meeting Ethan's gaze, her last sentence took on a new meaning. They both understood Tessa wasn't only referring to fillies.

He looked away and there was an odd tension between them. Uncomfortable, she asked, "So, what brings you here to the hospital? Did God whisper in your ear I was going to need backup?"

Ethan shifted uneasily as if guilty. "No. Mary had some papers that needed to be signed by me on society business. And since the clinic is on the way, I wanted to check on Hope and Lady, just in case the judge asks me about them. This judge sometimes likes to question different people about the animals' conditions."

That was a valid reason. "I just printed off the report, if you'd like to look at it."

"I would. Mary wanted me to remind you she wants you there in person at the hearing, in case the judge has any questions."

That wasn't an unusual request. "I can do that, but you'll have to tell me where the courthouse is located."

"It's in Los Rios. The hearing is ten-thirty."

"Okay, I'll be there, but I'll need directions." And she didn't want to repeat her mistake of getting lost on the rural roads. She only had to fall in a hole once to learn to be wary. Kind of like falling in love. She didn't need to repeat the mistake twice.

Ethan followed Tessa into the office. Doc Adams had brought in a battered metal desk and put it on the other side of the office from his messy rolltop desk. The computer monitor with hard drive underneath looked out of place in this room, which could've come straight out of a picture from a 1930s veterinary office. On the opposite wall, sitting on the metal desk, was a slick laptop. Tessa's diploma rested on the floor, waiting to be hung. Obviously, she hadn't had time to finish settling in. Between the two desks was a long table pushed against the back wall, with the printer on it. Underneath were several boxes.

"I haven't had time to unpack yet," Tessa explained, walking to the metal desk. "I'll need your email address so I can send you future reports."

"Agreed. I'll put you on the email loop for the Society. Now most of our ranchers have email, but I'll send you their phone numbers in addition to their email address."

"Thanks." She walked to the printer and picked up the report. Meanwhile, Ethan mentally ran over the information he expected the report to contain.

For the last day and a half when Ethan had been working at the ranch, he'd recalled Hope's birth. What an incredible moment. They'd snatched victory from the mouth of tragedy. When his parents asked about what had occurred at the seizure, the words came tumbling out full of enthusiasm and praise for the new vet, surprising his folks as well as him.

After he finished, his mother simply smiled her I-understand-what's-really-happening smile, while his dad shook his head. Their reactions puzzled Ethan but he'd been too distracted by thoughts of Tessa to dwell on them for long.

He felt as though he'd known Tessa forever.

That didn't make sense. He wasn't ready to feel such a strong sense of connection to a woman. He'd talked to God while riding out to check fences, but he hadn't come to any understanding of his feelings, even when he discussed his reaction with Ranger. He was glad his horse couldn't talk and comment on his odd behavior.

Adding to his turmoil, this morning Mary called, needing him to drive to Albuquerque to sign papers. He'd gone, but the tension in Mary's office was so thick, he knew that it was going to be a rough year while he was head of the rescue group. He couldn't fault Mary's legal expertise, but they'd never discussed what had happened the morning of their aborted wedding. Driving home from that tense meeting, he thought seeing Hope and Lady would be a good way to unwind. His anticipation had turned to alarm when he walked into Doc's medical barn and clapped eyes on Kevin Raney.

Ethan had had the unfortunate experience to meet Kevin years ago. Kevin had been traveling the rodeo circuit. He didn't rope or ride or participate in any of the events. What he did was provide drugs, drink, betting on rodeo events and poker games for the young men and the cowboys who worked the circuit. After a particularly ugly fight that had broken out among several cowboys, sending them to the hospital, Kevin had been barred from coming on the fairground or rodeo property. Later, Ethan had heard Kevin had spent time in the New Mexico state prison system.

So, what was Kevin doing with William?

"Here's the report," Tessa said, breaking into his thoughts.

His hand brushed hers when he took the pages. As if grabbing a live wire, a jolt raced through him. His gaze flew to hers. Her eyes widened and a startled "oh" escaped her perfect mouth. The surprise in her eyes told him he wasn't alone in the reaction.

The moment ended with the outside door slamming. Doc Adams appeared in the doorway.

"Hey, Ethan, what are you doing here?" He looked from Ethan to Tessa.

Ethan took a step away from Tessa and

turned. "I was driving back from the city and wanted to see how Hope and Lady were doing."

Doc gave him a funny look.

"After meeting with our lawyer," Ethan further explained, "I needed to spend some time with horses."

Doc's brow arched. "I see."

Doc's cryptic answer made the thirty-five-year-old Ethan squirm like he did the summer Doc had confronted him when he was sixteen and in a whole lot of trouble.

"It was fortunate he came," Tessa interjected. "There was a little difficulty with William and Kevin Raney."

"Oh?"

Tessa explained how Ethan's presence had resolved the situation with the men, making Ethan feel ten feet tall. Doc threw Ethan a glance. They both knew what trouble Kevin could be.

"Good thing you showed up," Doc said.

Did he hear something in Doc's voice?

"Yeah, it seems I've been doing that lately.

I'll see you on Friday at the courthouse." Ethan walked out of the office.

"Ethan," Tessa called to him, following him outside.

Stopping by his truck, he turned to face her. "Yes?"

"Thanks again for your help with William and Kevin." Her eyes softened with gratitude, making his chest tighten. "When you got here, I was wondering what I could do to stop them from taking Hope."

Her words sent a chill down his spine. "Be careful of Kevin. Despite the charming smile he so easily flashes, he's a con man, who's spent time in the state penitentiary some time back. And from what I've seen, I doubt that he's changed since he got out."

"Why was he in jail?"

"He ran a bookie operation."

"Gambling?"

"That's it."

"Thanks for the heads-up." The cold tone of her words could've frozen a side of beef in the middle of summer. "I've seen the destruction caused by it, so I'll make sure Kevin doesn't get his hands on Hope or Lady." Ethan was surprised by the vehemence of her reaction. Obviously, she had had some sort of run-in with a bookie.

"Don't try to take Kevin on. I can't guarantee he won't be violent. If it comes to your life or the horse's, you're more valuable."

The expression in her eyes mellowed. "I'll keep that in mind. Thanks."

Would she thank him if she knew why he knew that truth about Kevin? But there was no reason for her to know. His past mistakes wouldn't make a difference in their professional relationship, and that's the only kind of relationship either of them seemed to want. No doubt that was for the best. Anything else would only lead to disaster. He'd been down that road before and didn't like where it led.

The tiny town of Los Rios sported a beautiful courthouse, constructed in the late twenties, built in the Southwestern style using adobe and giant crossbeams.

Ethan had plenty of time to admire it as he sat beside Tessa and they listened to Mary Jensen summarize what they'd found at the ranch. Tessa had finished her testimony. When Mary was done the Moores' lawyer argued that the family had fallen on hard times. They hadn't meant to starve their animals.

The judge told them he would be back with his verdict in a few minutes. When he returned, he addressed the Moores.

"Doris, this is not the first time you've been before this court. But, this case is judged on its own merits. Seeing the pictures and listening to Dr. Grant, I'm awarding all the horses to the Rescue Society."

"You can't do that," Doris yelled, jumping to her feet.

The judge glared at her. "My ruling stands."

"What about the foal I sold?" she shot back.

"You'll have to pay the buyer back. If they aren't happy with that solution, have them file with the court for relief." The judge left the chamber.

The older woman turned, glaring daggers at the opposition table.

Tessa leaned close to Ethan and whispered, "Is she going to be trouble?"

"I don't know. She doesn't take defeat well."

Tessa looked at William, whose face had lost all color. "What about her son?"

Ethan didn't answer immediately.

"What do you think?"

"I hope he'll accept the verdict."

Tessa didn't like the sound of that.

"We'll just see," Doris muttered to herself. With a final defiant glare, Doris left the courtroom with William trailing behind her.

Ethan walked to the prosecution table and talked to Mary. From their body language, it was an awkward exchange. Mary Jensen was tall, probably five-ten, slender, with long blond hair and deep blue eyes. She was just the right height for the tall rancher who stood over six feet tall. With dark hair and steel-gray eyes, Ethan looked perfect with the golden woman. They were both smart, capable, cared strongly for the same causes. Tessa could see why they would have gotten together. So what had gone wrong?

"You ready to go?" Ethan asked, coming to Tessa's side.

Tearing her mind from her speculation,

Tessa gathered up her notebook and purse. "Sure, I'm ready."

They left the courtroom, heading for the elevators. Mary stayed inside the courtroom, packing up her briefcase.

After Ethan pushed the elevator button, he looked down at his watch. "I ate at six this morning and the cantina across the street has a great lunch special. You want to join me?"

Tessa opened her mouth to refuse when her stomach growled. She flushed.

"That's a yes if I ever heard one."

She was still tempted to refuse, but her stomach growled a second time, drowning out her pride. She'd eaten her breakfast earlier than Ethan and was hungry.

"Lead the way. But it's just a business lunch. We go dutch."

Ethan nodded. "Absolutely."

It was what she expected and demanded, so why did she feel disappointed he gave in so easily?

Chapter Four

"I couldn't believe Doris thought she'd get her horses back." Tessa reached for another tortilla chip and popped it into her mouth.

Ethan watched Tessa down the chips. The cantina stood directly across from the courthouse in the southwest corner of the square. As they'd walked across the street to the restaurant, he'd explained the Wednesday special was flautas, and they were some of the best he'd ever eaten. They'd both ordered the special.

Tessa picked up another chip and dipped it into the house salsa. "How she thought any judge would give her back those starved horses is beyond me. She had some prime horseflesh, an Arabian and a retired thoroughbred, and she starved them." She punctuated her comment by waving her chip around. A bit of the salsa landed on the table in front of Ethan.

Tessa stared at the blob. "Uh, I'm sorry."

"No problem." Ethan wiped the spot with his napkin, holding back a smile. The lady had a passion for horses and he liked it. And shared it.

"If she wanted to sell Hope, why not take care of the mare? What she did makes no sense."

He shrugged. "Doris didn't much care for her two children, neglected them, so why would she care for her horses?"

"Really?"

"Yeah." William and Shanna had often showed up to school in torn and dirty clothes.

Tessa fell silent.

The waitress appeared with their lunches. Ethan watched as Tessa tasted her food. After she swallowed, she grinned. "Okay, I have to agree with you. These are good."

As they ate, Ethan discussed how he'd notify the different ranchers caring for the horses that their organization now had legal custody. "I'll leave Lady and Hope with you, of course."

She nodded. "Okay."

He could tell something was on her mind. "Is something wrong?"

His question snapped her out of her musings. "No." She wouldn't meet his eyes.

He continued to study her. "Are you sure? Were you afraid I'd want to house Lady and Hope somewhere else?"

"No."

"It seems like something—"

"It's nothing." She waved off his concerns.

That was the worst denial he'd ever heard. "You might as well spit it out."

She thought about her question, pursing her lips. "There just seems to be a tension between you and Mary. And with what Kevin blurted out the other day—" Her cheeks flamed.

Well, he'd asked for it. Why not tell her? Everyone in this part of the country knew of his embarrassment, most people probably witnessed it. "Well—"

"Don't worry about it," she hurriedly added.

"It's not my business." Her weak smile tried to smooth over her gaffe.

She'd touched a raw spot. But with Mary back here, the talk would be everywhere and Tessa would hear about what happened sooner or later. He'd rather be the person who told her. "I was engaged to Mary."

"People break off engagements every day."

"True, but they don't leave the other person standing at the altar. Mary did." *Well, you certainly softened that, didn't you?*

"Oh." She turned a deep shade of red.

"All the people in this area were in the church that morning and witnessed it."

"I didn't mean to—"

He shrugged. "It was years ago. We were young and thought we were in love." He recalled with stunning clarity that humiliating morning, when he stood in the church with all his friends and neighbors gathered, waiting for the bride. After thirty minutes of waiting, her maid of honor showed up. She announced Mary wasn't going to show and handed him a letter.

Standing before all the people he knew and

had grown up with, he remembered reading those devastating words. Mary had written that she loved him, but not enough to marry him and spend the rest of her life with him. She felt she was too young and didn't want to get married. Besides, she wanted to go to college and see the world outside their little area of New Mexico.

Growing up on neighboring ranches, he and Mary were always at the same local events. They began to hang together and slowly became best friends after Mary's brother ended up face-first in a mud puddle at a local barbecue. They laughed at the same things and shared similar views. Everyone in the community thought they were a couple, and they were comfortable with the label.

He was a year older than Mary, and when he graduated from high school, he went straight to college. He didn't know if it was his going away and talking with other girls or that Mary had found someone new, but he noticed distance between them that first Thanksgiving he came home. He thought to solve the problem by proposing to her, which he did at Christmas.

The wedding had been set for the weekend after her high school graduation. Looking back, he realized Mary's calling off the wedding was one of the best things that could happen to him. He just wished she'd done it in a less humiliating way.

"Lot of people thought Mary and I were a perfect couple, but we were so young. I don't think we really knew what we wanted. Everyone told us we were in love, and we didn't know any better than to believe them." Looking back now, he could see that they'd just convinced themselves that they loved each other enough to marry.

"It must've been hard."

Something in her voice alerted him. He felt she understood his mortification. "Yeah, I took my share of licks here at home. Luckily in college, no one knew. And on the bright side, it certainly made graduating from college much easier without a wife to care for."

"I understand that. A couple of my classmates were married, but they were men. Their wives worked to help them through school. One guy was working and putting himself and his wife through school. He had to drop out for a year because of exhaustion." She fell silent, but he saw her thinking about something.

"Did you leave behind any special someone?"

"No." She said it with a vengeance.

"So, what's the story behind that 'no'?"

Her head came up and her shoulders tensed. "What do you mean?"

He raised his brow and his mouth turned down, letting her know he'd told the truth, now it was her turn.

She thought about it for a moment, then shrugged. "My senior year in college, I got engaged. We both applied for scholarships. I got one, he didn't. His solution to that was that I continue with the vet I was working for and support us while he went to law school. When he got his degree, he'd put me through veterinary school."

Ethan wanted to laugh, because he could guess what her reaction to that proposal would've been. "I assume you didn't take him up on his offer."

Her mouth twitched. "I considered it, but when I saw my fiancé having coffee with another woman, holding her hand and looking like a lovesick schoolboy, I knew what the score was. He was simply looking for someone to fund his law degree. And it wasn't going to be me." She toyed with her fork, pushing around her flauta. "It kinda took the bloom off the rose for me. After that, I was too busy in veterinary school to date. With my scholarship, I wanted to keep up my grades. I guess you could say I was single-minded on graduating."

He could understand her attitude. At least Mary hadn't tried to use him.

"Once the guys in school knew I was there for an MD and not an MRS, I didn't have problems with them wanting to date. They still wondered if I could cut it, along with my professors, but they watched, observed, then were okay with me."

He wondered if she lumped him in with that group of uninformed males.

The waitress appeared and they paid their checks. He walked her back to her car parked before the court building.

"Thanks for the help, Dr. Grant." He flashed a big smile.

"I think you can call me Tessa."

As she drove away, Ethan was surprised by Tessa's reaction to his being-left-at-the-altar story. She hadn't offered any platitudes, and no wonder. His experience with a broken engagement had been bad, but Tessa's experience was worse.

He found himself admiring Tessa. She fought for what she wanted and believed in and was even stronger after her broken engagement.

She might be only five feet tall, but she threw a mighty big shadow. And he felt himself responding to that amazing woman. With his history, though, he doubted she'd be interested in him. And oddly enough, that saddened him.

"How'd things go at the hearing?" Dr. Adams asked as Tessa walked into the clinic office. He sat at the rolltop desk, reviewing file folders. Doc still preferred the handwritten files that he wrote himself. None of his records were electronic.

"The Society was awarded custody of all the horses." She put her briefcase on her desk. "Ethan said he'd notify the different ranchers caring for the horses of the decision."

Doc turned in his chair. "Well, Lady and Hope are getting stronger every day. I expect that with good care and feed, the other horses should do as well."

"I hope so. Those horses were in bad shape. It might take a month to six weeks to get them in any type of shape to adopt."

Leaning back, he replied, "I agree," then asked, "How did Doris take the verdict?"

"She wasn't happy. I expect we might have trouble from her."

Doc sighed. "I don't doubt that. The woman is the most stubborn individual I've ever seen. Once she gets something in her head, she's like a dog with a bone. We'll need to be on our guard."

"I don't doubt that from her reaction in the

courtroom. Her son had to drag her from the court."

"Sounds like the Doris I know." He studied her and she tried to control her flush. "Did something else happen?"

"Nothing else that has anything to do about the court case."

"Oh?" He stabbed her with a look.

She didn't want to admit her misstep with Ethan but the question in Doc's eyes made her squirm. She'd learned early on how to put on a brave face to the outside world while things at home were falling apart. Her father's drunken episodes were never talked about at home or in public. After her dad disappeared, her mom and Tessa started back to church and found acceptance, love and compassion. With prayer, Tessa learned to trust others, although sometimes it was a struggle.

But Tessa knew trust between vets in this small a clinic was imperative and she needed to fess up. "I kinda stepped in it with Ethan. Last time Kevin was here he taunted Ethan about Mary. I noticed how tense they were at the hearing and asked him if what Kevin said was true."

A slow smile appeared on Doc's face. "How'd that go?"

"After I got over feeling stupid, Ethan told me about his broken engagement. I told him about mine."

"Oh?"

"It's an old story. My fiancé wanted me to pay for his law degree. I was to put my degree on hold, even though I was the one with a scholarship."

"Obviously, you didn't take the deal."

She laughed. The first time she'd ever laughed at the subject. "You've seen that play before?"

"I have."

"But when Ethan was talking about Mary, I got the feeling that there's something more—" She shrugged. "I shouldn't try to analyze him. I'm an animal doctor, not a psychiatrist."

Doc nodded. "Good call. I watched Mary and Ethan grow up. They were good friends, but there didn't seem to be that special spark that you want in a spouse." He shook his head. "Look at me.

I'm not a shrink, either, but common sense said they just needed to stay friends. It took a while after that 'almost wedding' for the talk to die down. Luckily, Ethan was away at school, and Mary was gone for more than ten years. She only recently has come home. Ethan hasn't said anything about it, but there's a tension. I know both Ethan and Mary are horse people, and they'll put the horses first and work together."

Tessa understood that passion. Growing up, she'd loved her horse. When her father lost their ranch, she asked the new owners if she could continue to board her horse there and work off Blue's board and feed. Eventually, they hired Tessa as a stable hand and paid her to work. She didn't go to high school football games or dances or her junior or senior proms. She spent those nights in the stables talking to Blue. Shaking off the bittersweet memories, she said, "Let me get changed and I'll check on Lady and Hope."

As she walked out of the room, she caught a glimpse of Doc's face. He smiled, a big satisfied smile.

Now, what was that all about?

* * *

Ethan slipped in the back door of the family ranch house that led to the kitchen. His mom stood over the sink peeling potatoes.

"Hey, son, how'd the court case go? Did the rescue group get custody?"

He leaned over and kissed his mother's cheek. In her mid-fifties, Lynda McClure was still a vibrant woman. She wasn't afraid to work outside with her children and husband on the ranch, but she also liked for her husband to take her into Albuquerque to see an art exhibit. Her zest for life made her seem years younger than her actual age. She was also a woman who could smell out a lie at thirty feet. Her children knew they couldn't pull anything on her, so it always amazed Ethan that she'd never probed his secret.

"It went well. The court awarded us custody."

"Good. I'm sure Doc's testimony helped." She pointed with her potato peeler. "Hand me those carrots."

He grabbed the bag and handed them to her. "Doc didn't testify. Tessa did."

"Oh?" She turned toward him. "How'd she do?"

"She did a great job. It was obvious the woman has experience in the courtroom testifying." Thinking about Tessa's testimony, he remembered the way she'd covered all the angles that the judge wanted to know. Judge Sanders had even commented afterward what a thorough job she'd done.

His mom's eyes narrowed. "That good, huh?"

Ethan immediately realized his mistake in showing too much interest. His mother's antenna was up. "Yes."

Lynda turned back to the sink, but he could feel his mother's smile.

"Don't get any ideas."

She didn't turn around. "I didn't say anything."

"No, but I know you. You're thinking it."

"You've turned into a mind reader, Ethan McClure?"

He heard the mirth in her voice. "I know you're itchy to get your last chick married off."

Turning toward him, she pointed her potato

peeler at him. "I think my son protests too much."

Ethan knew he was cooked. He leaned over and kissed her cheek again, hoping to distract her.

"What's that for?"

"Just because."

"What else happened?" his mother asked.

"Nothing."

"Your ears are turning red."

He grabbed a carrot and walked out of the kitchen and started toward the barn, not willing to talk about the lunch meeting afterward.

"Chicken," he heard his mother call out.

He smiled at his mother's accusation, and kept walking. Slipping into the barn, he saw one of the men who worked for the ranch. "Hey, Josh, how's it going?"

Josh Monroe had worked for their ranch for the past ten years. Before him, his father had worked on the ranch. Josh had ridden the rodeo circuit, but had been stomped by a bull and had to retire. He and his wife now lived in a house a mile or two from the main ranch house. When Ethan married, he planned to build his house not far from the main house, but close enough that he would be at the main house in five minutes.

"Everything's fine."

They spent several minutes discussing the different horses and Josh's plans to ride out to check on the cattle in Colorado Canyon and make sure all the calves were faring well.

Afterward Ethan walked out to the corral behind the barn. His horse, Ranger, and the rescued horse his family was looking after were out there. Ethan grabbed a couple of carrots. He called out to the horses and held up the carrots. Ranger immediately came and grabbed his treat. The other horse waited, watched, then when the gelding decided that Ethan wasn't a threat, he walked to the fence and took the carrot.

"You're looking better, guy. A little food and some TLC, and you'll be bouncing right back. I guess I need to give you a name." He studied the chestnut with black stockings, tail and mane. "You've got guts and a will to live, so how about Will?"

"You talking to the horses?" his dad asked.

He walked to the fence and looked out at the horses.

"Well, this guy doesn't have a name, and since the rescue group won custody, I thought I needed to give him one if he's going to be here awhile."

"I'm glad the hearing worked out. I heard Tessa dazzled the judge."

Ethan's head jerked around. "Who told you that?"

Ken's right brow arched. "Do you have to ask?"

He shook his head. "Mom. Well, the horses were starved. The evidence spoke for itself."

"Your mom got a different impression."

Ethan was sure she did. Turning, he leaned his arm on the fence. First his mother questioned him and now his father. What was going on here? Were they tag-teaming him? "If you knew about what happened, why'd you ask me?"

Ken looked out at the horses. "Why so grumpy?"

Ethan scowled, and stared at the rescued horse.

His father slapped him on the back. "You seemed unsure of Dr. Grant when she first showed up at the ranch. I'm just surprised you gave your mother a good report."

Ethan knew what his father was implying. "Well, you have to admit that you wouldn't have reacted any differently than I did if Chance had been the one who was being examined. I recall a certain farrier you threw off the ranch because you didn't like how he treated your horse."

"So what's that got to do with Dr. Grant?"

Ethan shook his head. His dad wasn't going to admit anything. "Yes, Tessa has proved herself competent with the birth, and her previous experience with horse rescue paid off at the hearing. She scored one for the good guys. But—"

"I'm glad you think so," his dad interrupted, "because Saturday, your mom has organized a dinner for the new doc to introduce her to all the local ranches. Both your brother and sister and their spouses will be there."

"When'd this happen?"

Ken lowered his head and stared at Ethan.

"Son, when has your mother ever told me about social stuff? She tells me where I'm going and I show up. It makes my life a lot easier. Remember that if you ever decide to make the plunge."

Ethan looked back at the horses in the corral. His dad slapped him on the back again. "I think your mother needs you up at the house." His dad turned away and whistled as he strolled back inside.

Ethan's gaze remained on the horses. For some reason, he felt unsettled, as if everyone else knew something he didn't. What was going on? His world had settled into a predictable pattern now that his younger brother had readjusted to life after his time in the army and losing his leg. It had been rough going, but now Zach was happily married with a wonderful wife and newborn baby.

Beth, his sister, had also taken the plunge into matrimony. Watching her grin and smile at her husband was both a joy and a pain. She'd been after him to find a wife. So he had both siblings in lovers' paradise, but he was alone, still living at home. Of course it didn't help that his ex-fiancée had reappeared in his life, silently pointing out to the community that Ethan was still single. He looked pathetic.

In his defense, he was taking over the reins of the ranch from his father, but on paper, things didn't look good. A thirty-five-year-old male living at home with his parents.

Normally, he didn't care what folks said, but inside he suddenly felt itchy. And he didn't know how to scratch that itch.

Lord, I don't know what's happening, but— give me guidance.

The image of Tessa's smiling face as she held Hope moments after that filly's birth appeared in his mind's eye.

"Son, you comin'?" his father yelled.

"Yup, I'm comin'."

Chapter Five

Tessa climbed out of Dr. Adams's truck and stared at all the cars parked in the driveway of the McClures' ranch. Tessa turned to Doc. "I thought this was just going to be a family dinner with the McClures."

"We've got several sets of McClures, plus their neighbors and friends, many of whom you've already met. Out here, we take any opportunity to get together and socialize. This is the West, Tessa."

She stared at him. Was this dinner just the cover for a surprise party? She hated surprises. Too often, her father had thrown surprises at them, which never turned out good.

Doc leaned close. "After spending all day

looking at only the back end of a cow or a horse, folks welcome dinner invites where we can talk to someone who will talk back instead of moo or whinny."

Tessa smiled in spite of her discomfort. "You mean that talking to your horse isn't enough?"

Doc shook his head and started toward the outdoor barbecue pit. Tessa reluctantly followed.

Several folks called out greetings. Doc waved and returned the greetings. He walked to the table set up with iced tea and cold sodas. Ethan stood there talking to a couple who held a baby.

"Zach, Sophie, Beth, Tyler, I want to introduce my new partner, Dr. Tessa Grant." He stepped aside and allowed the group to greet Tessa. "You met Lynda and Ken McClure at the clinic when you first got here. Zach and Beth are their other children."

Zach McClure shook her hand. "It's nice to finally meet you. I've heard a lot about you." He grinned at Doc. "I heard she's from your alma mater?"

"Indeed. Was a star in her class."

"And she helped on the seizure we did last week," Ethan added, joining the group.

Zach didn't look convinced. "Really? I heard you were—"

His wife shoved the baby in his arms. "Here, be useful."

He took his daughter and his expression softened.

Sophie stepped forward and offered her hand. "I'm glad you were here when that storm came through. We'd love to have you come out to the equine therapy ranch and watch what we are doing out there."

"Are you trying to steal away my vet?" Ethan asked.

Sophie's brow shot up. "Your vet?"

His siblings and their spouses stared at him. Ethan's ears turned red.

Tessa's breath caught.

Ethan stood up straighter, making his six-foot-plus frame seem even taller. "Yes, the vet for the rescue group," he qualified.

Beth and Sophie grinned at each other.

"What did you think I meant?" Ethan asked looking from one woman to another.

"Well," Sophie began. "It sounded like…"

Ethan waited.

"…never mind. Dr. Grant—"

"Please call me Tessa."

"Tessa, please come out to visit the ranch." Sophie told Tessa where their ranch was located. The baby in Zach's arms started fussing.

"Let me introduce you to everyone here," Ethan commented, cupping Tessa's elbow and guiding her away from his family.

"Why'd you do that? I'd have liked to hear more about your brother's equine therapy ranch."

Ethan ignored her question. "I thought you'd like to meet and talk to the other people who are housing the horses from our seizure. You didn't get the opportunity that night since you were so busy."

It *had* been busy that first night when the ranchers took the horses that Doc had seen and released. But somehow Tessa had the feeling that Ethan had other motives for pulling her away from his family.

Over the next few minutes, Ethan introduced her to every rancher at the dinner. Some she remembered, others she didn't. The welcomes Tessa received were mixed, but after news of Hope's birth, most of the skeptical ranchers seemed willing to give her a chance.

Ken rang the triangle hanging by the stone grill. "Dinner's ready, folks. Why don't we give thanks, then grab a steak and the other fixings and find a place to eat." Ken bowed his head and prayed over the food. "Lord, thank You for this bounty, these friends and Doc's new partner. Amen." He raised his head. "Let's eat."

It took several minutes for the crowd to get their meal. Tessa settled at the table with Ethan's family.

"Have you met everyone?" Beth asked Tessa.

"I have. And I talked with everyone who is caring for one of the horses we rescued. There are a couple of problems. I'll go out tomorrow and see about them."

"I do need to warn you about something." Beth looked around. "If either of them tells you something about me, don't believe it."

"Why is that?" Tessa asked.

"Because they're my brothers. Need I say more?"

Zach opened his mouth to protest, but Sophie elbowed him.

Beth laughed and Ethan grinned.

"It serves you right," Beth told Zach. She turned to Tessa. "Don't your siblings give you grief, too?"

"I was an only child." Tessa tried not to put too much emotion in her answer, but when she was growing up, she'd envied all of her friends who had brothers and sisters. Her childhood might have been easier with a brother or sister to share some of the hard times when her father would get drunk and claim her mom really didn't love him.

She felt Ethan tense beside her.

"I stepped in that, didn't I?" Beth gave her a sheepish smile. "Sorry."

"Don't worry about it. I had friends who wished they were an only child, but that's just part of growing up, wanting what the other guy has."

The conversation flowed easily around her. The teasing that went on between Ethan and his brother and sister warmed Tessa's heart. She felt the love flowing among the three.

"I hope you'll join us at church tomorrow morning," Beth added.

Tessa smiled. "I'd like that."

Beth and Sophie explained about the church and its beliefs.

"Sounds like a good fit. I'll need directions, but I'll be there."

"I have a better idea." Sophie glanced at Beth. "Ethan can pick you up and drive you to church."

Zach frowned. "But Dr. Adams—ouch." He turned to his wife. He reached down and rubbed his leg. "Why'd you do that?"

Beth bit back a grin while Zach looked at his wife.

The "ah-ha" expression that crossed Zach's face made his sister laugh. None of the men at the table smiled.

They looked at Ethan.

"Sure, I'd be happy to pick up Tessa," Ethan offered.

Tessa squirmed, aware of all the eyes now resting on her. "That's not necessary."

"You're right. It's not necessary," Beth said, "but I think it would be neighborly of Ethan to drive you to church. Don't you think so, Zach?"

Zach's eyes twinkled. "I do."

This was a losing battle and Tessa wanted to be gracious. "That sounds good. What time is the service?"

Ethan looked pointedly at his siblings. "Eleven, but Sunday school is at nine-thirty, so if I pick you up at nine, we can go to Sunday school and you can meet more of our neighbors."

Tessa felt the need for the fellowship and agreed. "Nine it is."

That night as Tessa was getting ready for bed, her cell phone rang.

"Dr. Tessa Grant."

"Oh, I never get tired of hearing that, sweetheart."

"Mom, are you back in the country?"

"I am. I just flew in from Brussels and my first thought was to call you. How are things in New Mexico?"

Tessa told her mother about her initial meeting with Ethan and the horse rescue. "You'd like Dr. Adams. He's a steady, calm man. And he trusted me and put me to work right away."

"I can't wait to come out there and see you. I should have a couple of weeks at the end of the month when I can get away. I also got a few more days of vacation along with a raise."

"That's great, Mom. You deserve it with all the work you've put in there."

"I might go on a Missions Trip later this year. Pastor Tim wants to finish working on the orphanage they started last year. Have you found a church yet?"

"Tomorrow, I'm going to church with Ethan."

"Oh? That sounds promising."

"Don't make too much of it. His sister and sister-in-law volunteered him." *But he is a nice-looking man,* she thought to herself, but didn't say.

"And what's this man look like?" her mother asked, seeming to read her mind.

"Mom, stop reading something into this. The man's six foot three and I'd have to stand on a ladder to ki—uh, see eye to eye with him."

Tessa had finally broken down and asked Beth how tall her brother was.

Her mother sighed. "Well, sweetheart, you're through school, got your veterinary degree, so it's okay to think about dating now."

"Mom."

"Don't let that selfish man who you were engaged to sour you on all men. You have to let go of the past, like I have. Not that I regret everything that happened—I certainly don't regret having you."

Tears clogged Tessa's throat. Her mother got pregnant her senior year in high school. Apparently, her parents didn't approve, because Tessa had never met her mother's parents. Her father's parents had died when Tessa was a baby and there'd only been her great-grandmother who hadn't been able to help much when her father walked out, leaving them with nothing. It had been a struggle and her mother always encouraged Tessa to get her education first before getting married. And the one time she was tempted, the guy shot himself in the foot. "Thanks, Mom."

"I want you to know, Tessa, I never regretted having you. You are the greatest blessing in my life."

Tessa's throat closed up with emotion. "Thanks."

"And as for the ride to church, I can't think of a better way to start."

A simple ride to church took on an entirely new meaning for Tessa. "Let me know when you're coming." After exchanging goodbyes, Tessa hung up.

Doc knocked on the door frame. "Is there any emergency?"

"No. It was my mom, checking on me."

He smiled. "Mothers do that."

"She was disappointed she couldn't help me move, but she was out of the country on a business trip for her company. She wanted to know how things were going."

"And you said?"

"I think things have gone well."

He nodded, folding his arms over his chest. Still a slim man, Doc Adams had a shock of white hair, vibrant smile and eagerly faced each day, but Tessa noticed the joints in his hands showed signs of arthritis. "I think I picked a winner. Good night, Tessa."

Tessa's heart swelled with pride. Most of the veterinary practices who dealt with large animals around her hometown of Lexington, Kentucky, didn't need another partner, especially one that was only five feet tall. No matter her ranking in her graduating class, they would only look at her height and wouldn't even give her an interview. "Lord, I was disappointed that no one in Kentucky wanted me, but I think You had a better plan for me. Thank You."

Life was looking good.

The next morning Tessa sat at the kitchen table drinking coffee. Doc wandered in dressed in jeans and a T-shirt. "You made coffee?"

"I also made an omelet. It's in the oven."

Doc grinned. "Thanks." He pulled the plate from the oven, and potatoes along with his omelet. "Tessa, you found my weakness."

A knock sounded.

"Not on Sunday, before my breakfast," Doc

muttered. Before Doc could move, the door swung open and Ethan walked in.

"Hey, Doc." Ethan looked at Tessa. "You ready to go?"

Doc glared at Ethan. "No, I just sat down to breakfast."

Ethan flashed Tessa a grin. "Not you, Doc. I'm here to take Tessa to church."

The look of irritation on Doc's face changed to surprise. "Why, I could—" He swallowed the rest of the sentence, looking from Tessa to Ethan. "I'm sure that Tessa will enjoy the service."

Tessa frowned. Something was afoot, but what?

Ethan stepped toward the door. Doc Adams dug into his breakfast. "Good job, Tessa."

"We'll see you later," she called out as she walked out.

Doc waved with his fork.

Tessa felt odd when Ethan opened the passenger-side door. She gave him a questioning look. He shrugged. "Blame my mother. She always insisted I open her door. I know you can do it, Tessa, but to make my mother happy, can we let this slide?"

Tessa wanted to laugh. "Okay, just you remember, I'm the vet."

"That's burned into my brain."

Tessa nodded and slid into the front seat. Ethan closed her door and walked around the front of the truck and got behind the wheel. Why did this suddenly feel like a date? They were just going to church.

As they drove out of the clinic parking lot, Ethan asked, "How'd you like our shindig last night?"

"It was nice to get to know your family. It occurs to me that the dynamics out here are different than city practice."

Ethan laughed. "Yup, out here we get up close and personal, but we also depend more on each other. You and Doc are our lifelines, so be prepared to become part of your patients' lives—or more accurately, the owners' lives."

Tessa hadn't really thought about that. That angle of this practice appealed to her.

"I think I'm going to like that part of rural practice. I think once the ranchers get to know me, they'll come to trust me, in spite of my size." She laughed. "I was really the odd man out in vet school. The other female students thought I was crazy to want to go into big-animal practice. At least the people here understand why I love big animals so much."

Ethan glanced at her. "So, I wasn't the only one?"

She understood what he meant. He wasn't the only one who was stumped by her choice of big-animal practice. "Unfortunately not. But after doing all the work in med school, why not go with what you love? And I think I have a way with horses."

"I'll give you that."

His answer surprised her. "Sometimes God drops something into our hearts and we know our call. I knew."

"Hey, I won't argue with God."

"Could've fooled me," she mumbled.

He shook his head as he concentrated on the road ahead. As they drove to church, she remembered how Ethan introduced her as Dr. Grant to the others last night. Tessa realized in that introduction was a note of respect.

That was a point in his favor. Maybe she was winning him over.

* * *

Ethan watched as Tessa's eyes widened when Doc Adams walked into the sanctuary. Doc grinned at them.

Tessa leaned over and whispered, "He goes here?"

Ethan tried not to smile. "He does."

She sat back and listened to the service. When they stood up for the scripture reading and prayer, she leaned close to Ethan and whispered, "I think I've been set up."

"If you remember, I wasn't the one who ramrodded this."

Tessa didn't know if she should be insulted, upset or perplexed. It seemed that Ethan's siblings were behind the push for him to take her to church. That thought discouraged her.

He added in a low voice, "I would've tried a different approach."

Tessa did a double take and her pessimistic view lightened. She felt unsettled and dizzy.

"You may sit down," the preacher said.

Tessa sat and scolded herself that she was here to listen to the sermon and see if this congregation was where she should be.

"In 1st Corinthians 8:35," the pastor began. Ethan opened his Bible to the scripture.

Tessa read the verse along with Ethan, but her brain was focused on what Ethan had just said. He would've found another reason to be with her. So his opinion of her had changed? There had been a note of pride in his voice when he introduced her last night.

A warmth spread through her chest. She tried to concentrate on the pastor's message, but kept thinking back to last night. A smile crept across her lips. Was he beginning to believe in her skills? Could be, but was there something else involved?

After the service, Ethan's family sought them out. She was introduced to dozens of people by Ethan and his family, in glowing terms. The ranchers she hadn't met before came by to say hi. That glow she felt earlier expanded. Doc Adams wandered over to where Tessa and Ethan stood. Her eyes narrowed on Doc. "You didn't tell me you came here."

"It never occurred to me. I was surprised when Ethan showed up this morning, but he seemed determined to be the one who brought you, so I let him. Besides, I wanted to finish the omelet. Good job, by the way."

"Well, I can go back to the clinic with you."

"Nope. I just got a call on my cell wanting me to drive out to the Jessup ranch and look at one of their cows. There's a problem. Ethan can take you home."

Ethan heard his name and turned back to Tessa and Doc. "What?"

"I've got a call. You take Tessa home." He didn't wait for an answer but simply waved and left the church.

Tessa turned to Ethan. "I smell another setup."

He leaned down and whispered, "It's easier to go with the flow, than to have my family try and try again to throw us together. Why don't we take the reins and decide what's right for us?"

She liked the sound of that. "For today."

He raised his hands. "I'm only going to take you back to the clinic, with maybe a stop for lunch."

With work waiting for her at the clinic, she

preferred to eat out. "Okay, but remember, today's okay isn't tomorrow's."

As they finished their lunch at a small trendy hamburger joint on the southeast edge of Albuquerque, Tessa's phone went off. Ethan watched as she talked with the rancher on the other end.

"Okay, I'll be there ASAP." When she hung up, she turned to Ethan. "I need to get out to the Barlow ranch. Apparently, William showed up at their place, trying to take one of the rescue horses. As he was trying to load the animal, the horse cut his leg on some metal on William's trailer. The horse got away and William drove off. I need to get out there. Can you drive me back to the clinic so I can get my bag and truck?"

"Sure." Ethan left enough money for both of their lunches. When Tessa started to object, he shook his head. "For a new visitor to church, it's my treat."

"This time only."

He mumbled something under his breath

that sounded like "being plagued with stubborn females."

They drove back to the clinic and Tessa got her gear together in less than twenty minutes. Ethan waited for her.

"Do you know the way out to the Barlow ranch?" he asked.

She stopped dead in her tracks. She'd met the Barlows last night, and knew their ranch was close to the McClures' place, but she'd never actually been there. "Actually, no."

"Follow me."

"Thanks."

She tried not to think about anything but the roads they were driving as they made their way to the Barlow place. When they arrived, Steve Barlow had the horse in a stall and his leg wrapped. One of the sheriff's patrol cars sat beside the house. Steve and his wife and the deputy waited outside the barn.

The instant she walked through the doors, Tessa forgot all the people standing around watching her. "Did you see this happen?" she asked Steve.

"As we were driving in from church, we saw

William struggling with the stallion. When he saw us, he tried to force Samson into his trailer. That's when the horse cut his leg. He reared and William let go, jumped into his truck and drove off with his trailer empty. It took us several minutes to chase this guy down."

Knowing how traumatized the horse was, Tessa calmly approached the animal. "How are you doing, big guy?"

The animal backed up, his head high, his eyes wild. Tessa stopped and studied the animal. Steve Barlow had managed to wrap a towel round the stallion's foreleg, but blood kept trickling down his leg and he was shaking.

It was a standoff. She started to croon to Samson. He stopped shaking and allowed Tessa to come close. She took her time letting the animal get used to her. Once the horse accepted her touch, Tessa went to work, all the people watching her forgotten.

Tessa's wonderful way with horses still awed Ethan. She was a natural. Each time he watched her work, his respect for her grew. When she asked for his assistance, he knew the woman put the animal first and wasn't into grabbing the glory for herself. Watching her, it was obvious she loved her work. He understood her on a deeper level.

When Tessa finished, she rubbed the horse's nose. "You were so good. And despite your injury, you're looking better, big guy." She turned to Steve. "You've done a great job with him. I'm sure it hadn't been easy. This guy's got to be part Arabian."

"I agree. And I can see why William wanted him back. He's a little high-strung, but I think with care, he'll settle down. Why don't you come into the house for a cup of coffee?"

Ethan waited for her response. In the city, she'd immediately leave, but out here in the West, it was important that the vet take the time to get to know the ranchers.

Her eyes flashed to him, then back to Steve. "That sounds good. Thank you."

Ethan breathed a sigh of relief. The lady had good instincts, with horses and people.

As they walked to the house, he fell into step

beside Tessa. "Good move," he whispered out of the side of his mouth.

She didn't respond, but continued walking.

In the kitchen, the deputy sat at the table with Connie Barlow, drinking coffee. They joined them, and the deputy questioned Steve as to what happened. Next, the deputy asked about the condition of the horse.

"He'll recover fairly quickly. A week ago, before the Barlows started caring for him, I would've guessed that horse would face major complications. Now, with just a week's care, I think the horse will do well. The Barlows have done a wonderful job."

Ethan watched in amazement at how Tessa worked her charm with the Barlows as well as the horse she'd just worked on.

If he wasn't careful, Steve, Connie and the horse wouldn't be the only ones Tessa Grant worked her charm on.

And he needed to remember that she was a professional woman, and he'd already had his brush with a woman who wanted a career.

Chapter Six

Tessa sat at the kitchen table with a cup of coffee. She'd worked in the hospital all morning, inputting their files into the computer and updating the Rescue Society's records. Doc, who declared he wasn't going to deal with the paperwork since he had a partner, used an emergency call from one of the neighboring ranches, about a cow that wasn't eating, to escape.

The past two weeks had sped by, but the problem with William showing up to bother other ranches where rescue horses were housed hadn't died down. The sheriff went out to the Moore ranch a couple of times but William wasn't there and Doris stood at her door with a shotgun. That worried Tessa. She recognized the look of desperation in William's eyes the last time he was here. She'd seen it often in her father's eyes when he came home after losing money.

Tessa ran her hand over her cup. She'd taken a break, gotten coffee, read her Bible and prayed. Now, she was taking a moment to stare out the window and enjoy the scenery. It surprised her how much this place, so different from the rolling, green hills of Kentucky, had settled into her soul. She liked the cool nights and warm days. Aside from slathering her lips with lip balm, the lack of humidity also appealed to her. Her hair loved it.

Grabbing her coffee, she walked through the stables to the corral where Hope frolicked. Lady, the mare, had recovered nicely from the birth. Her coat was filling in and her weight had increased. There was also more vigor in her gait. Hope also was flourishing, her injured leg healing. Soon, there would be no limp.

Tessa sipped her coffee and enjoyed the antics of the foal. "Oh, you're going to be a handful," she told Hope. "We've got to get your momma well so she can guide you."

"She sure is looking good," Kevin Raney commented, coming around the side of the barn. He strode up to the corral fence and flashed Tessa a slick smile.

Her spine stiffened.

"You've done a good job with that little filly."

"What are you doing here?" Tessa demanded.

"Well, I thought I'd like to pick up my property."

Tessa remembered her cell phone on her desk in the office. "The court awarded the Society custody of all the horses. At this point, you probably need to contact either Ethan McClure or Mary Jensen about that."

"Hey, I'm here with my horse trailer, and I could just load her up now. The Society took her away from William and Doris, but they have no reason to keep her away from me."

"Hope is still nursing. Are you willing to bottle feed her?"

He shrugged. "Whatever it takes."

What a fib. "If you're going to petition the court for custody, you're going to need to show you're willing to take care of the horse. I think even the Society would work with you if you showed them a bill of sale."

His smile vanished to be replaced with a narrowing of his eyes.

"I don't think he has a legitimate bill of sale, do you, Kevin?" came Ethan's voice from behind them.

Tessa and Kevin looked at the barn doors and saw Ethan striding toward them.

"Huh?" Tessa looked from one man to another. "What are you talking about?"

The men glared at each other.

"You going to fill in the lady or do you want me to tell her the truth?" Ethan asked Kevin, coming to Tessa's side.

Kevin continued to glare.

"I'll take that as a no." Ethan looked at Tessa. "If I don't miss my guess, Hope was in lieu of a gambling debt that William owed to Kevin."

"Oh." Tessa had been down that road before and it hadn't ended up well. "It doesn't change my answer. Take it up with the court or the Society."

Kevin glared at both of them, then turned and stomped off around the side of the barn.

"I'll be back in a few." Ethan followed Kevin around the building. He returned in less than two minutes.

Tessa let out a breath. "You must be listening to God closely, because you've shown up here at critical points. I don't know what I would've done if Kevin had insisted on taking Hope. My cell phone is sitting in the office."

"I can't claim divine inspiration." Ethan moved to Tessa's side and studied the horses in the corral. "Doc called me this morning and asked me to pick up some medicine and feed while I was in town. I've got it in the truck. When I saw Kevin's truck and trailer parked in front of the clinic, I came looking."

"Why do you suppose Kevin is so persistent?"

"I don't know, but I think that's a question the sheriff needs to ask."

She'd faced this kind of trouble before— gambling trouble.

The clinic phone rang. Walking back into the barn, Tessa grabbed the barn extension on the wall. "Dr. Grant."

"Dr. Grant, this is Steve Barlow. It seems that the tin of salve you left is missing. Would you have another one?"

"I do."

"I'll come and get it later."

Tessa glanced at Ethan. "I've got a better idea. Ethan is here. I'll send it with him and that way you won't have to make an extra trip." The call quickly finished. When she hung up, Ethan gave her a questioning look. "I have a job for you." She explained the situation.

"So could you take the medication out to the Barlows for the rescue horse?"

"Sure, I can do that."

She walked to the cabinet in the corner of the barn that held the medical supplies. She grabbed the step stool and climbed on it to reach the salve on the top shelf. As she reached for the small metal tin, she felt Ethan reach around her and grab it.

Turning her head to say thank-you, she came eye to eye with him. She forgot about the medicine and looked into Ethan's face. The air seemed charged with electrical energy. Ethan's eyes darkened, then his gaze slid to her lips. His left hand came up as if to cup her cheek.

The sound of the screen door slamming jerked them apart. Tessa started to lose her balance. Ethan caught her arm, steadying her.

"Am I interrupting something?" Doc Adams asked, standing at the entrance to the barn.

Ethan turned to Doc. He held up the metal tin. "Tessa was getting medicine for me to take out to Steve Barlow."

Tessa nodded, then slowly stepped down.

After a moment of awkward silence, Doc asked, "Ethan, what are you doing here?"

"Delivering your order."

Doc looked chagrined, running his hand through his hair. "Yeah, I remember now."

"I was glad he showed up." Tessa explained about the run-in with Kevin.

Doc's expression turned stern. "What's going on? I've heard from several ranchers about William and Kevin showing up, causing trouble. We can't be locking the horses up every time we walk out the door and the other ranchers are getting fed up with those two clowns messing with their stock."

"I agree," Ethan said. "Why don't we go inside and notify the sheriff?"

When Ethan started toward the door leading to the breezeway separating the house from the hospital, Tessa held back.

Ethan looked over his shoulder. "Are you coming?"

"Give me a second." Her heart continued to race and she wanted to be settled before she talked to anyone about what happened.

Ethan started toward her. She held up her hand. "It's okay, Ethan." His indecision was written clearly on his face. "Please."

Her plea worked. He nodded and walked out of the barn.

Her stomach still danced, but she guessed it wasn't from the encounter with Kevin. No, it was that almost-kiss. Her mind had gone on vacation, leaving her heart in charge. That traitorous organ had urged her to lean forward and meet Ethan's lips.

What was going on? Her brain needed to come back home and take control before—

"Tessa, I've got the deputy sheriff on the phone," Doc Adams called out. "Hustle in here. I need you to talk to him."

She raced into the kitchen, but she doubted she could outrace her feelings.

Doc didn't speak, but Ethan knew he was mad. Doc dialed the sheriff's office. "This is Doc Adams." He glared at Ethan and held out the phone. "Talk."

Ethan took the phone and answered the questions the deputy asked. "You really need to talk to Dr. Grant to see how the incident started." Ethan waited for Tessa to take the phone.

While she chatted with the deputy, Doc pulled Ethan aside.

"What's going on?" Doc demanded.

"What do you mean?"

The older man's brow arched. "When did you suddenly quit understanding English?"

Ethan shrugged. "I was getting salve for Steve to use."

Doc's eyes narrowed.

"Nothing happened." The explanation sounded like an eight-year-old defending himself.

"But if I'd had come in two minutes later, you couldn't claim the same thing, could you?" A muscle in Doc's jaw jumped.

Why explain the obvious?

Doc searched Ethan's expression. Doc had been there when Mary stood him up.

"Since I know you, son, I'm not going to object, but if you run her off, I'll skin you."

Whoa, Doc was serious. "I'll do my best to live up to your standards."

Doc nodded toward Tessa. "I think I've got a winner there."

"Thanks, sheriff." Tessa hung up the phone and turned to the two men. "He told me to be careful and carry a phone at all times. He also asked if I know any self-defense moves."

"Do you?" Ethan asked.

"Yes. After a couple of incidents on campus, the university offered self-defense classes with one of the local police instructors. Besides, I went to vet school surrounded by lots of guys. I picked up a few techniques."

Her answer didn't ease Ethan's mind. "But

I want you to know that Kevin's been known to be armed most of the time."

"If I run into him again, I'll let him take the horse. I won't act like a hero."

Somehow, Ethan didn't see Tessa giving up so easily.

Doc stepped to Tessa's side. "I hope you're leveling with us, because I've discovered I like having a partner—especially a partner like you."

Tessa's expression softened. "Thank you."

"I'll be back in the office, charting what I did this afternoon."

"You should try using the computer," Tessa answered. "I've tried updating the files. And if you use the computer, I won't have to worry about reading your writing."

"I'll consider it." He nodded to Ethan.

They watched him walk out of the house down the breezeway into the hospital unit where the records were kept.

"He may not be up on the latest computer thing, but he's an amazing man," Ethan said.

"You two are close, then."

"We are. I visit Doc as often as I can. I

worked for him between my junior and senior years in high school here at the clinic and learned a lot from him."

"So that's why you're so good in assisting me."

He grinned.

"I worked in the stables all through high school, too." A look of sadness settled over her face.

"Didn't you like it?"

Her eyes widened. "Of course I did, why would you ask?"

"You just seemed sad."

Tessa stiffened. When he thought she wouldn't answer, a strained laugh escaped her mouth. "I spent my junior and senior proms at the stable with my horse and the other horses, working. And I was happier in their company than I would have been with any boy in my high school."

There was more to the story. "Were the boys so bad that you'd prefer horses to them?"

Her eyes twinkled. "I hadn't thought of it that way, but yes, they were. The horses certainly were better listeners and didn't ask stupid questions."

She started back into the stables.

"Whoa, you can't leave me hanging."

She grinned. "Sure I can."

"You drop a bomb, then walk away." He found he wanted to know more about her. "What's that?"

"There's nothing to tell. I worked with a stable manager all through high school. All my free time was spent there, but oh, the education I got. Old Tom—which everyone called him— helped me develop my ability to understand horses. And horses were great company for a fourteen-year-old girl whose world blew apart."

Ethan followed along behind her. He understood that sentiment. Horses could soothe your soul and could bring peace in a storm. He'd done his share of "talking" to horses as well as talking with God when his world turned upside down.

Looking out the open barn doors, he saw Lady and Hope and Tessa walking to the corral fence. The incident with Kevin blazed across his mind and he knew something needed to be done about William and Kevin. Luckily Doc had cell phone reception here at the clinic. He pulled out his cell phone and called Mary, telling her what had happened. He walked to the corral beside Tessa.

"I understand the board needs to talk about it. Why don't we call a meeting for tonight at the Bar-T Restaurant?" he suggested.

"Isn't that kind of expensive?" Mary asked.

"It serves first-rate steaks and since we're all paying for our own, I doubt any of the board members will object to eating a good meal before we deal with this problem."

He heard Mary tap a pen or pencil on her desk. "Can't do tonight. How about tomorrow? I won't be able to file papers until Monday, anyway."

"Sounds good."

"Will you contact all the board members?"

"I'll do it." Ethan put his phone in his shirt pocket and walked out of the barn, stopping at Tessa's side. "The board's going to meet on Saturday night to discuss the situation with

William and Kevin. I just talked Mary into holding it at a nice steak place in town."

"A steak place?"

"If we're going to have to deal with this situation, we might as well reward ourselves with a good steak. It helps the brain."

"I hadn't heard that explanation before."

Ethan grinned. "Well, you haven't practiced too long out here. If you want, I can pick you up. That way you won't have to worry about driving to a new place in Albuquerque at night."

Tessa considered the invitation.

"We all need to hear of the incidents and your input will help the board."

"Wouldn't Doc be better for this?"

"I'd like to have his input, but you've been most directly involved. You need to be there."

"I'll talk to Doc about it. I think he might like a good steak dinner, too. I could ride over with him."

"Then it's settled. Let's tell Doc, then I'll unload the supplies Doc asked me to get."

As he drove home, Ethan tried to ignore the emotions rolling around in his chest. Fear for Tessa, disappointment she didn't want to ride with him and unease at the prospect of spending time with Mary. For so long, his heart had been encased in ice. Now that it had thawed, he didn't know what to do with any of the feelings swamping him, threatening to drown him.

He didn't want to have this battle now, but he didn't have a choice.

When Tessa walked into the kitchen, Doc was sitting at the table.

"I thought you were going to update your files," Tessa said, pouring herself a cold glass of tea.

"I did."

"On the computer?"

"I turned it on, but didn't fight with it. What were you and Ethan talking about out there in the barn?"

She explained about the board meeting.

"A board meeting at the Bar-T? Smart man."

"Why do you say that?"

"Because Ethan knows that's how he'll get all the board members to agree to go to that meeting. They all want an excuse to eat steak."

"I'm guessing you'll take the excuse, too? I told him you should be the person at the meeting from this office."

Doc stabbed her with a look. "Why's that?"

"You've dealt with William longer than I have."

"But it's your problem, too, Tessa. You've got to stand up for yourself and come up with an idea on how to deal with this situation. If you're going to be doing your share of the practice, people have got to know you can pull your weight. Tell Ethan it will be only you at the meeting. And it'll probably be easier if you let him drive."

Doc's reasoning made sense. She needed to step up and deal with the situation. "Okay. I'll let him know, but in the meantime, let's go put your updated files on the computer."

Doc frowned.

"You want your clinic as up-to-date as possible," she offered. "Once you're familiar with it, I think you're going to like it."

"The jury's out on that one."

"You just haven't had the right teacher.

C'mon, let me introduce you to your computer."

"I'd rather face the south end of a north-bound mule."

Tessa laughed, wishing her dad could've been more like Doc.

Later, Tessa called Ethan. "Doc's not going to come to the board meeting, so to save myself the embarrassment of getting lost, I'd like to take you up on the offer of driving me there."

"I can do that."

To Tessa's amazement, he didn't make an issue out of it. "Then I'll see you Saturday at—?"

"Five-thirty," he supplied. "That will give us plenty of time to get to the restaurant."

"Thanks, Ethan." She hung up. Feeling unsettled and anxious about the board meeting, Tessa called her mother.

"Hey, sweetheart, how are things going out in New Mexico?"

"Great, Mom." She talked for a while about how much she was liking the area, and how welcoming nearly everyone had been. "Of course the story on how I delivered Hope put me in a good light with the ranchers." But then she explained about the problems they were having following the initial rescue.

"If Ethan hadn't shown up just in time today. I don't know what I would have done."

"Ethan?" Her mother paused. "Ah, yes, I think you mentioned him before."

Of course she had. "He *is* the head of the local rescue group." Why did she feel defensive?

"What do I hear in your voice?" her mother asked.

"What are you talking about?"

"There's a lightness in your voice when you mention that man."

She must've put more emphasis on his name than she intended. "Ethan is, well...he doubted my skill, but I think I'm starting to win him over."

"Oh."

"As a veterinarian, Mom, nothing more. That's why he asked me to the Society business meeting."

"Really?"

The more Tessa talked, the worse it sounded. Her mother always knew when she had good news or bad. When she'd called after breaking up with Brent, her miserable fiancé, Tessa only had to say "Mom" for her mother to know something was wrong.

"Trust me, Mom, it's nothing more than a board meeting."

"Tessa, you don't have to defend yourself to me. I've prayed that what happened with your father, then Brent, didn't turn you off the idea of falling in love. There are good men out there."

"Mom, it's a board meeting. Nothing more."

"Really?"

The more Tessa talked, the deeper the hole got.

"Tessa, you know I felt guilty about—"

"Mom, I don't blame you for Dad's drinking and gambling. He did that. As for Brent, I kinda knew something wasn't right for a long time. I just didn't want to admit it."

Tessa heard her mother sniffle. "I'm glad things are working out at that clinic for you.

That people are accepting you and you're working with the Rescue Society. Do you really like being out West? I worried that maybe you wouldn't like the area."

"I love it, Mom. I want you to come out to New Mexico as soon as you can to see for yourself what a great place this is and meet the people."

"I'll try, sweetheart. I think I'll be able to come maybe around Thanksgiving. We got a contract with that company in Brussels that we're having some trouble with. I'm going to be going back and forth several more times." The talk shifted to her mother's work for a while before both of them had to admit they were tired. After saying their goodbyes, they hung up.

Tessa couldn't wait for her mom to meet Doc Adams and the McClures. Disappointed her mother couldn't come for the next several months, Tessa comforted herself with the fact her mother had finally won a big promotion in her company.

As she got ready for bed, Tessa thought about the call with her mom. Odd, it sounded as though her mother was in a parking garage. Maybe her mother had worked late again and Tessa caught her going home.

Drifting off to sleep, she heard her mother's warning not to let her father and ex-fiancé ruin her future. Surely her mother would understand the wisdom of guarding one's heart against heartache again. Surely she would understand.

Surely.

Chapter Seven

Saturday morning, Ethan drove out to his brother's equine therapy ranch after getting Zach's panicked call, asking if he would come and help. One of the horses had gone lame, several of the volunteers hadn't shown, and the baby and Sophie were sick. The world was coming to an end and Zach couldn't think. Ethan readily agreed.

On the drive to the ranch, Ethan thought about the most recent incident of Tessa confronting Kevin. He'd had nightmares about it last night. Since he'd found that small woman in his stables examining his horse, he'd felt off his stride. Really, his world had tipped off its axis.

After Mary left him standing at the altar, he'd been gun-shy about commitment. Sure, he'd dated casually in college, but nothing ever clicked. Over the past few years he occasionally went out with the few single women from around here, but they knew about his aborted wedding and viewed him more as a friend… or sometimes as "poor Ethan." He could have done without the pity but in a way it had been a relief that no one expected him to put his heart on the line again.

Was he ready now?

"Lord, I don't know what's happening, but guide me, because I'm on ground I haven't ridden on before."

He checked in with Zach when he got to the ranch. The baby had a slight fever and Sophie was asleep, having spent most of the night up with the baby. Zach looked completely beaten.

As Zach looked down into his daughter's bed, he turned to Ethan. "I think I'd rather lose my other leg than have that little one get sick again."

Ethan shook his head, because he knew his brother was in for a lot of sleepless nights in the future and lots of time spent in prayer. Not voicing his opinion, Ethan hurried down to the stables. On his way there, he called his mom and apprised her of the situation. She was on her way.

"Morning, Ollie," Ethan called out, walking up to the stables.

The old foreman grunted. "You here to help?"

"I'm the cavalry coming to the rescue. What do you need done?"

"What I need is five more people and someone in the office to answer the phones. I ain't no secretary. If you want nice talking, then get someone else."

"Is Beth here?"

"No."

Ollie was in a mood this morning. Since he wasn't any better a secretary than Ollie, he called his sister. "Can you come and help out? We're short of people."

"I can and I'll bring Tyler with me."

"Thanks, sis." Over the past month, Beth and Tyler had resettled into a new home in Albuquerque. Tyler had worked at the ranch for close to a year, living in the foreman's house. But after Tyler and Beth married, they moved to the city, making it easier for Beth to get to work and the airport for her frequent business travels. Tyler had signed up with the city to become a policeman.

When Ethan walked into the stables, he saw Tessa examining Dakota, a two-year-old gelding.

"Funny meeting you here like this."

Tessa looked up from where she squatted by the horse's left foreleg. "The clinic got a panicked call from your brother. What are you doing here?"

"I got the same desperate call." He squatted by Tessa's side. "Zach's baby and wife are sick, and the man is a basket case."

They smiled at each other.

She patted Dakota. "Cut your brother some slack. New parents are cautious with their first arrival."

"Somethin' got to account for his odd behavior."

"What in the Sam Hill are you two doing down there?" Ollie demanded.

Tessa stood. "Well, it looks like Dakota stepped on something, a rock, or something hard. He'll need to be on restricted movement and to be kept on a soft surface. It doesn't look like there's any infection, but keep an eye on him. And no riding him for a few days."

"What else can go wrong?" Ollie grumbled as he walked away.

"Is he always so charming?" Tessa asked, watching the old man disappear around the corner.

Slowly rising to his full height of six-three, Ethan smiled down at her. "Sometimes he's more abrupt, but we love him like that. When Ollie came up with cancer and was nice to all, it had us worried. I'll take his bad moods any day."

"That's a positive way of looking at things." She ran her hand over the horse's shoulder.

Ethan grabbed Dakota's lead rope and led him to the back corral. When he came back inside, Tessa had finished packing up her equipment.

"Can I pick you up about five-thirty this afternoon? That should give us plenty of time to get to the meeting."

"Sounds good. See you then."

As he watched her go, he reminded himself this was a board meeting, not a date.

At five-fifteen Tessa walked out of her room into the kitchen where Doc sat doing charts— paper charts. She wore a simple sleeveless black jersey dress, black heels and a long string of pearls. Earlier she'd had on jeans and a Western shirt, but Doc informed her that the restaurant was a dress-up place.

Doc looked up and paused. "Well, you clean up nice."

"Do I look okay for the meeting? I mean, this isn't a date. What will the other board members think?" She pulled off her pearls.

Doc grinned. "They'll think you knew the dress code for the restaurant. I'm sure several of the other board members' wives will be there in their Sunday best."

Tessa walked to the table and eyed the folders. "Am I ever going to get you to use the computer?"

Holding up his hand, Doc defended himself. "I wanted to write these notes before I try typing them in. I only want to worry about one thing at a time." The man grinned, making the corners of his blue eyes wrinkle. With a full head of white hair, he was still an attractive man, but it was obvious he'd spent his life outside from the weathered condition of his face.

"That's a good idea."

"What's a good idea?" Ethan asked, opening the back door.

Tessa started to frown at the man for always showing up unannounced, but then her eyes took him in. Dressed in new creased jeans, white shirt and a tan sports coat cut in Western style, and boots, he looked so good that she couldn't form any words. In his right hand, he held a tan Stetson.

Ethan whistled low, then stopped himself, looked at Doc Adams, then back at Tessa. "Uh, I didn't mean—" He swallowed. "Nice dress, Tessa."

Tessa's heart skipped a beat. "Doc told me about the dress code at the restaurant. I hope this is okay." The pearls in her hand slipped.

Ethan caught them and handed them back to her. "Yes." He waited for her to put the pearls on.

Doc shook his head. "Get out of here."

Ethan flushed.

"I guess I should say 'don't keep her out too late.' You never know when we might have an emergency."

"Got it." Ethan escorted Tessa to his truck and held open the passenger-side door.

Once on the road, Ethan flashed her a smile. "If it makes you feel any better, I got the third degree from my parents before I left. Wanted to know where I was going and with whom." He shook his head. "When I said a board meeting for the Rescue Society, they gave me an odd look. I told them where it was and Mom still was acting weird."

Strange, Tessa had the same feeling with Doc Adams, as if he was seeing her off on a date. That was an experience she'd never had with her father, since he'd split long before she was old enough to date.

But she wondered, if her father would've

stuck around, would he ever have smiled at her as Doc did? And would she have felt as proud?

The board met in a separate dining room at the back of the restaurant. Once all the board members arrived, they ordered dinner and ate. Tessa took the time to ask each of the ranchers how their rescue was doing. After the last plate was cleared, the board began serious discussion on the situation. Finally, Mary said, "So it's agreed that I need to file a restraining order against both Kevin Raney and William Moore."

"Agreed," Ethan said and all the other board members concurred.

"Then I'll do it first thing Monday morning." She put her pad away in her briefcase.

"Everyone, be sure to report any further trouble with Kevin or William," Ethan instructed. "We want as much documentation as we can get for the restraining order."

The meeting broke up.

As Mary talked with the Cousinses, Mason Lee, one of Mary's law associates, introduced himself to Tessa. He explained that he was going to start working with Mary on Society business.

"Do you think it will be hard to get that order?" Tessa asked Mason.

"No. Mr. Raney is a familiar name around the courthouse. He's been connected with a lot of defendants in swindling and running book, but no one's been willing to roll on him."

Ethan heard the last of the exchange and stepped close to Tessa. "So the man hasn't changed. It's good to know what we're up against. We'll be extra careful."

With a final goodbye, Ethan escorted Tessa to his truck. Her silence as they left the city made Ethan wonder what she was thinking.

"I'm hoping that the restraining order helps," Ethan said, "because I don't want to see any more of our volunteers hassled."

Tessa came out of her musings. "I hope so, too. You've got a lot of good people in your group."

"I think you've won over most of the board. Steve Barlow told me he thought Doc had found a good one with you."

Her smile glowed in the dash lights.

Ethan found himself telling her stories about different ranchers who were there. He told her how Steve Barlow ended up proposing to his wife, Connie, over the PA system at the state fair one year.

"He didn't." Tessa laughed.

"He did. She was all over the fair, doing everything from helping with the 4-H lamb judging, to entering her pie in the cooking contest. He tried three times during the fair to propose, but was always interrupted, so the last night, in frustration, he walked to the PA booth, explained to the announcer what he wanted, and they let him take over the PA system and ask her. He met her in the middle of the arena, put the ring on her finger and kissed her, in front of all those folks."

"I don't know if that's romantic or what." Tessa laughed.

"Well, it was the horse rescue that brought them together." Ethan glanced at her. "So why did you get into horse rescue?"

"I love horses, and when I was in high school, the place where I worked took in a rescue horse. I cared for that gelding and watched him go from a wounded creature who didn't trust anyone to a healthy horse and a wonderful animal. The owner gave the horse to his granddaughter and a happier pair you've never seen. It was then I knew the power in rescue. I wanted to do more." Every word she uttered resonated in his soul.

She studied him. "What about you? Why are you in rescue?"

"Doc Adams got me into it the summer I worked with him. He was passionate about it and, just like you, I saw the difference it made." And it made up for the mistake he'd made. "Ranger was a rescue. He was my first rescue."

"I can see why you were a little edgy that first time you saw me with him."

When they pulled into the parking lot of the clinic, a brand-new red Ford F-150 SuperCab sat before the clinic doors.

"I wonder who's here at this time of night," Tessa said as they came to a stop.

"I don't know. I don't recognize the truck. And it still has dealer tags on it." He hopped out of his truck and ran around the front of his vehicle and opened Tessa's door. As they passed the new truck, Ethan got a good look at the paper tags. The dealer was in Kentucky.

Tessa opened the screen door to the breezeway and walked inside. The overhead light in the breezeway was off, allowing them to see clearly through the glass window in the kitchen door. A handsome woman with pixie-style brown hair sat at the table with Doc. He sat with his back to the door.

"Do you know who the woman is sitting with Doc?" Ethan murmured. "I've never seen her before, but she seems familiar."

"Mom," Tessa whispered.

His eyes widened. Mom? He looked from the woman to Tessa and saw the resemblance.

Tessa opened the door and rushed into the kitchen. "Mom."

The woman stood and opened her arms. Tessa ran into them.

Ethan grinned and looked at Doc. He wasn't smiling. There was a grimness around his mouth and eyes, which set Ethan back on his heels.

"What are you doing here?" Tessa asked when she drew back to look at her.

"I'm bringing my daughter her graduation present."

A gasp escaped Tessa's lips. "That new truck I saw outside is for me?"

Her mother nodded her head. "I've been planning this for the last six months. The dealer kept the truck for me while I was in Europe, and when you called yesterday, I was in Missouri eating lunch on my way here. I hoped you wouldn't guess."

"Oh, Mom." Tessa threw her arms around her mother again.

Tessa turned to Doc. "I guess you've met my mother."

He nodded. "I have."

Her mother's eyes went to Ethan. "And this is…"

Tessa gasped and turned toward Ethan. "Mom, this is Ethan McClure."

Her mother's brow arched, making Ethan curious.

"Ethan, my mom, Joan Grant."

Ethan shook her hand. "It's nice to meet you, ma'am. Your daughter's made quite a splash."

Joan cocked her head. "I sense a story."

"I'll say she made a good impression on my horse." Ethan and Tessa laughed. Doc smiled.

Tessa waved away the story. "Let's go see my graduation present." She hurried outside to the parking lot with everyone trailing behind her.

Tessa stood staring at the truck for a moment before she ran her hands over the front fender. "My old truck's going to be jealous."

Did he hear right? "Your truck has feelings?"

"I talked him through the last winter at school and he didn't fail me."

Ethan grinned and turned to Doc. Oddly, Doc looked torn, as if he didn't know whether to laugh or cry.

Tessa ran her hand down the side of the truck, around the back, and came up to the driver-side door.

She opened the driver's door and stepped up on the running board. The seats were leather, with all the bells and whistles inside—GPS, radio/CD player, everything anyone could want. "Oh, my, Mom, you put all the good-ies in this."

"I did," Joan answered.

Looking inside, Ethan whistled. "That's a top-rate setup."

Tessa slid into the captain's chair and ran her hand over the dash, then leaned her head on the steering wheel. "You must've saved for a long time."

Joan smiled at her daughter. "I think you deserve this with all the work you've done." She opened the passenger door of the truck and pointed to the dash. "One of the perks I had them add was heated seats."

Tessa stared at her mother. "Really?"

"Absolutely." Her mother slipped into the passenger seat. "There were too many times that you had to do without and you never com-plained. I wanted to give you this now because I could."

Ethan glanced at Doc. The older man's mouth was turned down in a frown.

"Besides," Joan continued, "I thought with the weather in Kentucky or wherever you ended up, you'd need the extra heat if you got called out in the middle of the night during the winter, or early in the morning."

"I like that idea," Ethan commented, thinking of the cold mornings he drove out to meetings or out to deliver feed on the range. "It won't take long for you to find the benefits of heated seats living around here."

Tessa beamed as if it were Christmas morning. "Well, I'll just have to drive my present to church tomorrow."

Ethan said his goodbye, then pulled Doc aside. "Is everything okay?"

Doc frowned. "Everything's fine. Why?"

"Well, you look a little out of sorts."

"You're imagining things." Doc stomped away.

After saying goodbye to Tessa and her mother, Ethan headed home. Seeing the joy in Tessa's eyes as she hugged her mother and investigated her graduation present, he knew that whether he liked it or not, his heart was involved with a five-foot dynamo who didn't know the meaning of the word *no*. She'd overcome the odds against her. But could she overcome his wariness when it came to relationships?

What a surprise Tessa's mother had been. Giving her daughter a new truck was one of the best gifts he'd heard about.

But as he thought about it, he wondered at Doc's tempered reaction to Tessa's reunion with her mother. Was he mad that Joan showed up unannounced? That didn't make any sense. Doc wasn't a prickly kind of guy. Then what was the cause of his odd reaction?

Was something going on that he should know about?

Tessa watched as Ethan drove away from the clinic. Turning back to her mother, she felt a blush rising in her cheeks. "The truck is a dream, Mom," she said, trying to dispel the odd feeling running up her spine.

Her mother beamed. "I got it for you because we've made it, sweetheart, despite the odds."

Out of the corner of her eye, Tessa glanced at Doc, who stood in the breezeway. His bleak expression surprised her. She didn't think he minded her mother visiting, so why did he have that expression?

"How long are you going to be able to stay?" Tessa asked, as they walked inside.

"I'd planned on staying for a week. I wanted to have some time with you since we haven't had some really good mother-daughter time since you started school."

Most of Tessa's vacation time for the past few years she'd spent at stables where she'd housed her horse or the veterinary practice close by. "Great."

Later that night as they were getting ready for bed, Joan walked out of the bathroom, rubbing lotion into her arms and said, "So that's Ethan."

Tessa looked up from the journal she was reading, putting her finger on the line where she stopped. Apparently, she'd put more in her voice when talking about Ethan than she realized. "Yes, that's him."

"So tell me about him."

She explained about the McClure family, Ethan's reaction to her caring for Ranger, and

Hope's birth. "I think after he's worked with me, I've won his respect. And—"

Her mother sat on the edge of the bed and waited for Tessa's answer. "And what?"

She ran her hand through her hair. Tonight, something changed between Ethan and her that she couldn't identify. "I don't know. I'm just—" her mind searched for the word "—aware of him. It's something I've never experienced before."

Her mother leaned forward, resting her elbows on her knees. "You get that tingly feeling in the pit of your stomach when you're around him."

How'd she know that? "That's it."

Her mother's eyes went soft and her lips curved slightly upward. "I know that feeling."

Tessa had never seen her mother with that expression on her face before.

"It was that way for me with your father. If he walked into the room, I knew it. We laughed and found joy in just walking in the park or sitting in lawn chairs and looking at the sky. Of course, that was all we could afford."

Tessa gaped at her mother. Never had Joan mentioned falling in love with her father.

"It was a wonderful summer." Joan seemed to come back to the present. "I understand those feelings."

Tessa wasn't ready to acknowledge "those feelings," so she turned the focus back to her mother. "You've never told me about how you and Dad fell in love."

Joan stared down at her hands. "It was a long time ago."

Tessa waited. "I'm not that old."

"True." Her mother thought about it, then nodded. "It was the summer between my junior and senior year in high school. I was at the local burger drive-in, having a root beer float. He was the new guy working in the kitchen. I saw him through the window and caught my breath. Later that day, I found an excuse to go back to the drive-in without all my friends."

Tessa had never seen that relationship between her parents. By the time she could remember, there seemed to be a strain between them.

"He noticed me, and after his shift, he

bought me a shake." Her mother shook off the memories. "And the rest is history."

It hadn't all been a good history, though it was nice to hear her mother still had some pleasant memories. To change the subject, Tessa set aside her journal, swung her legs over the side of the bed and grabbed her mother's hands. "I'm so glad you're here to see where I work so I can to share it with you.

"Doc Adams has been great. He's treated me as a partner from day one. Of course the man is old-fashioned but if I can get him in the twenty-first century with computers and doing things the easy way, I think he'll like it."

"So, he's been fair with you?"

Tessa sat next to her mother. "He has. More than fair."

Joan slipped her arm around Tessa's shoulders and drew her close. "I'm glad things have turned out so well."

"I think you'll be impressed with the ranchers around here when you meet a lot of them tomorrow at church."

Her mom nodded, but there just seemed to be something off about her reaction. Tessa didn't understand, but decided not to push and ruin the precious time she had with her mother.

But sleep didn't come quickly as she couldn't keep the doubts at bay.

Chapter Eight

Tessa bounced into the kitchen the next morning. Her joy and excitement at having her mother visiting buoyed her spirit. The new truck sitting outside the kitchen window only added to her elation. "Good morning," she cheerfully greeted everyone.

Her mother sat at the kitchen table, a cup of coffee in her hands. Doc sat across the table from Joan with his own coffee. Between them was an apple streusel coffee cake, given to Doc yesterday at Llutz family ranch. Ranchers in the area kept them well stocked in baked goods. Tessa had joked with Doc the first time he came back to the clinic with a brisket, asking if that was the payment. He simply smiled.

When Joan looked up to greet Tessa, for an instant Tessa saw a deep sadness in her mother's eyes. Instantly it disappeared. "Hello, sleepyhead," she teased.

Tessa kissed her mother's cheek, wondering if she'd mistaken the sad expression. Could her mother miss her that much? She'd been away from home for the past eight years getting her DVM degree. That didn't make sense.

"That looks great, Doc." Tessa nodded to the streusel, then walked over to the coffeemaker and poured herself a cup. When she turned around, she caught Doc stealing a glance at Joan. Tessa couldn't interpret Doc's expression. She joined them at the table.

Tessa cut herself a piece of the coffee cake and put it on one of the napkins in the center of the table. Taking a bite, the flavors of cinnamon, sugar and apples burst onto her tongue. "Oh, my."

Her mother and Doc smiled.

"As far as I'm concerned, Mrs. Llutz can pay in pastries from here on out."

"Tessa always lived on her stomach. My little girl wasn't afraid to chow down."

Doc laughed, but there was that hint of melancholy in his eyes.

Although it was a joke that Tessa never left food on the table, there had been times when there wasn't anything to eat. Love and understanding filled Joan's eyes.

"Greta has a gift for cooking," Doc added. "And you'll find the residents of this part of New Mexico are very proud and will always pay whether in trade or money. You won't often get a thank-you or approval after you've doctored one of their animals, but they'll pay in one way or another." Doc took another sip of his coffee. "One time, I had one of the ranchers tell me he'd pay me throughout the year with hay once his crop was harvested." He shrugged. "I didn't have to buy hay the next year. Same with Stan down at the garage. I saw his daughter's dog—"

Tessa arched her brow.

"I do treat dogs and cats. Anyway, the dog had heartworms. The treatment was expensive, but Stan serviced my truck until he paid off his debt. That's how things work out here."

Joan smiled. "It's not only out here. Farmers

in Kentucky and in the Smoky Mountains do it, too." She nodded at Tessa. "Ask your new hire there."

Doc turned to Tessa.

"I had a horse. Things got tight when I was growing up and when we couldn't pay for the horse's feed and stabling, I went to the stables and offered to work free in exchange for my horse's room and board. The owners agreed."

Doc glanced at her.

"I wanted to keep my horse, and thought of a way to do it."

Approval shone in the older man's eyes. "I knew I liked your style when I interviewed you on the phone."

The compliment warmed Tessa's heart. She felt her mother's glow of pride.

She glanced at the clock. "Oh, I've got to see to the horses before we go to church."

"Not a problem," Doc answered. "I fed them. You just get ready."

Tessa sat back in her chair. With the exception of her mother, Tessa had never been able to count on another person to take up the slack in her duties. She felt tears sting her eyes. "Thank you."

He nodded, acting as if it was nothing special. "And I think you should drive that new truck of yours. Show it off."

"But I don't have my equipment transferred over."

Doc smiled. "Don't worry. I'll drive mine, just in case we have an emergency."

Tessa liked the idea. How thoughtful of Doc. It was a new experience for her to have a man show consideration for and pride in her. What would it have been like if her dad had been like that?

After the church service, Ethan's family gathered around Tessa's new truck, oohing and aahing at the beautiful vehicle. Several of the ranchers that Tessa had already dealt with also came by to admire the truck. She felt like a new mother, showing off her baby.

"It won't stay new-looking long," Steve Barlow drawled. "Looks mighty nice now. Enjoy."

Everyone laughed.

"I think I need one of those vehicles," Ken

McClure stated, once the crowd had diminished. "It even has seat warmers, doesn't it?"

"It does." Tessa grinned at her mom. "And I'm going to enjoy them, particularly on those winter days when I've got an emergency."

"And in the dead of the night," Doc added.

Lynda McClure stepped forward. "Tessa, why don't you and your mom come and join us for lunch?"

Tessa opened her mouth to refuse, but Lynda held up her hand. "I've made enough to feed an army and both my Beth and Sophie are coming, and bringing food. Remember, this is the only socialization we get. Please come. We'd love to have you and your mom join us."

"What about Doc?" Tessa asked.

"Not to worry. He has a standing invitation to come to lunch every Sunday. He'll be there." Lynda glanced at Doc. "Won't you, Vince?"

"I wouldn't miss it." Doc turned and headed for his truck.

"What do you think, Mom?"

"I'd like that."

"And you can share the dirt about Dr. Tessa," Beth teased.

"There are stories," Joan replied.

"Mom!"

Joan tried to look innocent.

Tessa could only pray her mother didn't pick anything she couldn't live down, because there were some doozies.

While the men sat in the den watching a pre-game football program, the women organized the food and placed it on the table.

Joan thanked Lynda again for the invitation.

Lynda waved off the comment. "We're so glad that Doc found a partner and a talented one, too. Doc's been our vet for the last twenty-some-odd years." Lynda lowered her voice. "The man's not moving as fast as he once did, and we encouraged him to bring in another vet." Lynda looked at Tessa. "She's not quite what we expected, but I think she's going to work out fine."

Joan studied her daughter. "She worked hard for that degree. If she hadn't had the scholarship, she couldn't have gone."

"You must be proud."

"I am."

Lynda grabbed the platter of brisket and walked to the table. "Lunch."

The men filed into the dining room. When Zach started to sit by Tessa, Ethan gave his brother a dark look. Zach shrugged and sat by his wife. Tessa looked around at the seated couples, Zach and Sophie, Beth and Tyler, Lynda and Ken, Doc Adams and her mom. She stopped there, looking at the two of them.

"Let's pray," Ken said.

He offered a short prayer for the couples at the table, the abundance of food and for God's grace.

"Amen," they said in unison.

As the dishes were passed around, Ken asked, "Joan, what do you do?"

"I work for Kingston International. I started as a secretary and worked my way up to VP of my division." Her mother described the company and what they did.

Afterward, the talk turned to horses and the equine therapy ranch. Everyone had a story to tell about their adventures with horses.

The laugher and fellowship around the McClure table made Tessa yearn. This is what a family should be, with jokes and smiles, shared concerns and prayers, instead of sullen meals with a father who was either too drunk to appreciate the meal, or too animated, his breath smelling of whiskey. Tessa watched as each of Ken's children joked and talked with him. He knew about their lives and asked questions and offered help. It was Tessa's dream of a family.

She traded glances with her mother and knew her mom had the same thoughts.

Not only was the happy family dinner a new experience for Tessa, her awareness of Ethan was a first for her. She never had this "awareness" before, even with her fiancé, and kept on thinking of things she wanted to ask Ethan, or things she wanted to tell him.

Ethan leaned close and whispered, "Don't let the arguing fool you, they love each other." Zach and Beth had been arguing about how stubborn she was and how she'd made her brothers' lives miserable.

"I'm not fooled," she answered. "I see the love."

"Good." He nodded. "And you be sure to put

in a good word for Zach and me to my sister. Bethy needs to appreciate us."

"Not a problem."

Ethan raised his voice and pointed at Tessa. "You need to chat with Tessa, Beth. She can give you a better perspective on your brothers. One that'll help you appreciate us."

Beth rolled her eyes. "In your dreams."

He shrugged and leaned toward Tessa. "See what Zach and I have to put up with?"

Beth wrinkled her nose at him.

"I need to hear this, too," Zach added. "I don't think I've been appropriately appreciated."

Beth held up her forefinger. "I think you have. There was a certain incident the night of the football game with Mesa Heights High School your senior year that still remains a secret. I can share…"

"Okay, Beth, you win." Zach grinned at his sister.

Folding her arms over her chest, she nodded. "I thought so."

Laughter rolled around the table.

Midway through the meal, Doc got a call.

He excused himself and walked into the living room. "I can be there in twenty minutes," Tessa heard him say. When he reappeared, he explained that there was an emergency at the Randalls'.

"I'll come with you," Tessa offered.

"No. You won't have your mother here often. Besides, I've had experience with this particular cow before. She loves eating that loco weed." He shook his head. "Stay here and enjoy dessert."

They quickly finished the meal. After dishes were cleared away and coffee brought out, Lynda brought out a large dish of banana pudding. "Sophie fixed this. And if you don't want pudding, I think Beth brought her brownies."

"I'd like both," Ken said, causing the men to agree with that sentiment.

Sophie studied her sister-in-law. "Beth seems to be on a chocolate jag—she brought chocolate cake last Sunday."

"And the week before that, when we were making s'mores, I caught her inside eating the Hershey bars," Zach added.

Everyone looked at Beth as if waiting for her

to announce something. She stood and said, "What?"

"Since when have you been a chocoholic?" Zach asked, his voice full of suspicion.

Beth grinned. "For about the last few weeks."

Lynda looked at her daughter. "Really?"

Beth nodded.

Her mother squealed and hugged her daughter.

Ethan frowned. "What's everyone yelling about?"

Zach looked at his brother. "Think, O Single Man."

The light came on for Ethan. "Oh."

Ken grinned. "So I'm going to be a grandpa again?"

"I haven't been to the doctor yet," Beth explained, "but according to the store-bought test, yes. I'll go Tuesday morning for the official verdict."

The women laughed and cried and made a fuss over Beth. When Tessa's eyes met Ethan's, her heart fluttered in her chest. And she thought she saw something special in his eyes that made her heart dance in a way it never had before.

After lunch had been cleaned up, Ethan used the excuse of having Tessa check the progress of the rescue horse to escape with her. His mother just grinned at him.

Mumbling to himself, Ethan walked with Tessa out to the corral where the horses were.

"He looks good," Tessa said, watching the bay with black stocking on his legs. "He was in the worst shape of all the horses, besides Lady. You've done a good job."

"He doesn't miss a meal, that's for sure." Ethan rested his arms on the top rail of the enclosure. "And the farrier came on Friday morning to get his feet in shape."

"Ranger's healing well, too, along with Ringo and Sadie."

He nodded and looked out at the other horses in the corral.

As Tessa turned toward him, the wind caught several strands of her hair, blowing them into her face. Ethan reached out and tucked the strands behind her ear. Their gazes held.

She swallowed. "Thanks for making my mom feel so welcome."

"I think my mom, sister and sister-in-law wanted to get the dirt on the new doctor from a close source." He grinned.

"That's a good idea. I wonder what kind of dirt I could get on you," she shot back.

He shrugged. "I'm sure my sister would be willing to spill her guts. As I said before, she liked to snitch on both of her brothers."

She rolled her eyes. "Probably with good reason."

Holding up his hands, he surrendered. "Okay, truce."

"As I thought." She turned back to the corral. "What's the real reason you brought me out here?"

His heart raced. You'd think he was fourteen, wanting to hold a girl's hand. "I wanted to see if you'd go out with me."

Tessa went still, remaining silent, which only added to his edginess. He thought things went well the other night. Sure it was a board meeting with other folks there, but it made him want to have a real date. At least he thought he wanted a date. One minute he thought asking Tessa for a date was a good idea. The next, he didn't know.

"What do you have in mind?"

"The rodeo is in town this weekend. I thought you might like to go and see it. Besides, I'm going to compete."

"You're what?" She turned to face him.

"Well, when I was a teenager, I rodeoed. They're having a roping competition for us over-the-hill guys and I signed up." He shrugged.

"Over-the-hill?"

Was that a smirk?

Leaning against the corral, he ran his fingers through his hair. "They're defining it as men who hadn't competed in the last eight years."

"So you're an old codger?"

"I'm starting to rethink this. Maybe having you witness my humiliation might not be the best idea I've ever had."

She waved away his last words. "Oh, no, you can't back out now. I'd love to go and see you compete."

He searched her face, weighing her answer.

"Okay, the prelims are on Friday night and the finals will be held on Saturday."

"So is this a date for two nights?" she teased.

"Only if I make it to the finals."

"I think I might like that." Her eyes twinkled with delight.

Ethan felt that smile way down in his gut. He prayed he didn't end up eating dirt and leaving his pride on the arena floor.

"Then I'll see you for sure on Friday night about five."

"I'm looking forward to it."

Ethan hoped she felt that way at the end of the night.

The call came into the clinic just after noon on Wednesday. Tessa took it.

"Tessa, this is Mary Jensen. Could you meet me at the courthouse by three this afternoon? I'm going to talk to the judge in the Moore case. Things got crazy at the courthouse and they postponed my Monday hearing and rescheduled it for today. I want you to tell the judge how much improvement the horses have made. I think your testimony before the judge impressed him. I also want you to tell the judge how William and Kevin kept harassing the animals and the people caring for them. I want all the ammunition I can get."

"Sure, I can make it."

"Good. See you at three."

Tessa made it to the courthouse just in the nick of time. She joined Mary and the judge in his chambers. The restraining orders were quickly granted.

As they headed toward the elevator, Mary asked, "Would you like a glass of iced tea at the restaurant across the street before we drive back? They also have great flan and pralines."

Thinking that Mary wanted to discuss more Society business, Tessa agreed.

Once they were settled with the iced teas, Tessa asked, "What other Society business do you want to talk about?"

Mary looked directly at Tessa. "It wasn't the rescue group I wanted to talk about exactly. I guess you know that Ethan and I were once engaged."

Tessa squirmed. "I heard that."

"Yeah, it isn't a secret. I ended it kind of publicly. For years, I've felt bad for Ethan that he had to stay here and deal with the fallout...to be the focus of all those pitying looks."

"Then why did you do it?" The words shot out of Tessa's mouth, surprising her. But now that they were out, she wanted to know the reasons Mary had stood Ethan up.

Mary leaned in and dropped her voice to a whisper. "He was my friend, Tessa. My best friend, but I didn't love him like I should. I wrestled the night before our big day with that very question. I prayed and I knew I couldn't go through with the wedding. It would've slowly choked me—us. We would've both been miserable and ended up hating each other.

"I had a drive to go to college, then to get my law degree. That was the most important thing in my life at seventeen. I didn't want to be married or be a rancher's wife. There's nothing wrong with that, but that wasn't what I wanted—who I am. I wouldn't have been happy. Can you understand that?"

Tessa took a sip of her tea and considered. If Mary had made any other argument, Tessa would've blamed her. But she'd been in a similar situation. "More than you know. That desire to go after the life I wanted drove me during my undergraduate years and veterinary school. It's deep inside."

"Exactly. I wanted to talk to Ethan about it, but when you're that age, you're lucky to know what you want to wear the next day, and he seemed so set on finishing college and coming back here to ranch. I doubted he would've understood my goals." She shrugged and fell silent.

Listening to Mary was like hearing herself. Tessa was older when her fiancé gave her that bad option, but she still understood Mary's feelings. Knowing Ethan as she did, she doubted he would've told Mary to blow her dream off, but it's hard to have perspective on those things when you're still a teenager. "I understand your dilemma."

Mary sat back and relaxed. "You do?"

"I do. I called off my wedding, but long before we got to the church."

Mary toyed with her tea glass, moving it around in circles. "I did the right thing, but I just did it the wrong way. My only defense is I was young and scared."

"Have you told Ethan this?"

The glass quit moving. "No."

"I think it would make things easier for you both."

Mary's eyes met Tessa's. "You're right."

The admission surprised Tessa.

"You may not believe this, but I'm glad Ethan's interested in you. Also, if you're going to be working with the rescue group, I wanted to lay my cards on the table with you. Clear the air."

Tessa started to protest Mary's statement that Ethan was interested in her, but he'd just asked her out and she'd accepted. Still, Mary's words unsettled Tessa. "You don't harbor any feelings for the man?"

"Oh, I have feelings for Ethan, but they are just feelings of friendship, combined with good memories. He's the most levelheaded man I've ever known. He sees things I don't, and I think he'll help my cases for the Society." She laughed and shook her head. "I might have to pay him a retainer as a consultant.

"I hope you'll accept my good wishes."

Tessa scrambled to gather together some coherent thoughts. "Well, I don't know if there's a relationship or not at this point, but thank you."

"It's nice to see my old friend have a goofy grin on his face again."

That alarmed Tessa.

As she drove home, Tessa kept reviewing the exchange with Mary. Tessa understood completely Mary's dilemma of marrying too young. It hit too close to home. But what really shook her to the core was Mary saying Ethan had a goofy grin on his face when he looked at her.

Was she ready for that? Was she ready to put her heart on the line again? It'd been disastrous the last time she'd tried. Could she do it again? Did she want to?

Having her mom with her this week had been a blessing. It was the first time since her father left that Tessa had spent any serious time with her.

Doc, her mom and Tessa took turns making

breakfast during the week. It was nice having food waiting for her the days she didn't cook. The only cloud on the horizon was the tension between Doc and her mother. Early in the week, Tessa just chalked it up to her mom being in a new place and Doc not used to having females in his house, clinic and barns.

But instead of the tension easing, it seemed to notch up every day. Tessa worried over the situation but couldn't reach any conclusions. Friday morning, Tessa left her mother in the bedroom as she finished dressing.

"Good morning, Doc," Tessa greeted. "What's on the agenda today?"

"I'm due to go out to a couple of ranches, but I plan to spend the rest of the day trying to update my files on the computer."

Tessa raised her brow. "You know, if we had the right kind of phones, we could actually access those files in the field." She grabbed up two coffee cups. "Do you want me to pour you a cup, too?"

He looked up from the pan of scrambled eggs he had cooking on the stove. "I do."

Grabbing another mug, she poured three

cups. She put cream and sugar in her coffee. The other two she left black. She leaned back against the counter and sipped her coffee. "Do you mind my mother being here?"

Turning his head, he asked, "Why would you ask that?"

She looked down into her cup. "There seems to be an awkwardness between you and Mom, and as the week's progressed things haven't eased. In fact, the tension seems to have gotten worse. Are you angry with her for some reason?"

His head jerked around to stare at her. "Of course not." He turned off the gas burner and carried the pan to the counter where the plates rested. He dished out the eggs. "I didn't even know who your mother was until she drove in here the other night with your truck. I think you're imagining things."

"What's Tessa imagining?" Joan asked as she walked into the room.

Doc put the pan on the stove and turned to her. "She thinks there's a tension between us."

Joan's eyes widened. "What? You're imagining things, Tessa. What would make you think that?"

Tessa looked between her mom and Doc. Neither one spoke.

"There seems to be a strain between you two. Am I wrong?" Tessa prayed she was.

A look of panic darted across Doc's face.

"Tessa, I think you're borrowing trouble." Joan grabbed her plate from the counter and brought it to the table. "Now, let's eat. I'm starved." She sat and opened yesterday's paper, which had arrived in the mail, and started reading.

Doc followed Joan's example, and pulled his notes close to review them. Obviously, neither one planned to give her a real answer. Something was afoot, but what, she didn't know. Her mother was the master at hiding bad things from Tessa. She prayed now wasn't a time her mother was hiding the truth.

Chapter Nine

As Tessa went about her day, the situation with her mom and Doc kept nagging at her. It put a damper on her anticipation about the date tonight with Ethan. When he arrived at five to pick her up for the rodeo, she laughed at the horse trailer attached to his truck.

"It's going to be the three of us on this date?" she asked, walking out of the walkway door.

"It is. I need Ranger for the calf roping."

"Well, I can't think of a nicer third on a date. I guess there's some sort of poetic justice about bringing a horse on a date with a veterinarian."

Doc and Joan came outside.

"Good luck, Ethan, with the calf roping," Doc called out.

"Mom, you sure you don't want to see the rodeo?"

"I think dragging your mother along on a date isn't what Ethan wants." She nodded toward him. "His horse is enough of a chaperone."

Tessa fought her mirth. "Uh, Doc could take you."

If she'd asked them to jump off the roof of the stables into a pile of hay, they would've had the same expression.

Doc was the first one to recover. "If Ethan makes it into the finals, I'll bring your mother tomorrow night," he promised.

"Deal." Tessa kissed her mom on her cheek and slipped into the passenger side of the truck.

Ethan waved at Doc and Joan as he pulled out of the clinic. After a moment, he breathed a sigh of relief. "I wasn't planning a double date."

His quip caught Tessa by surprise. She looked and him, and they both broke out into laugher. She laughed so hard, her sides hurt and her stomach ached.

"Okay, I was pushing it," Tessa admitted. "But there was a reason behind my madness."

"And that was?"

Tessa knew she needed to talk to someone about the situation with her mom and Doc, and with Mary's endorsement of Ethan's level-headedness, he was the perfect person to voice her concerns. "There's an odd tension between my mother and Doc. I thought it was just the strangeness of the situation. Doc's not used to living with two women. But as the week's progressed, instead of relaxing around each other, the opposite seems to have happened and the tension is worse today than when Mom first showed up."

Ethan's eyes darted to her. "That doesn't sound like Doc. He's usually friendly with everyone. Did you ask him about it?"

"They both denied anything was wrong. Said I was just imagining it. I do a lot of things, Ethan, but dreaming up fantasy scenarios isn't one of them. It's driving me crazy. It's like walking around waiting for an explosion."

He remained silent, but she could see from the set of his chin that he was considering various options. "Maybe they don't like each other. Of course, Joan would be the only person I know who doesn't like Doc. Aside from that, maybe they aren't comfortable with each other and are trying not to poison the relationship between you and Doc. It would make things harder for you. From what I've seen of your mother, that's the last thing she'd want to do."

Tessa thought about it. "Could be, but I remember Mom had a manager she worked under who she didn't like. The woman returned the feelings, but Mom endured the woman for close to a year without any real awkwardness until Mom got promoted to another department and didn't have to work with that woman anymore."

Ethan glanced at her. "A couple of months ago, Pastor preached a sermon about praying blessings on those who you work with and you have a problem with. Pastor added that usually God changes our heart and rearranges our attitudes, so maybe your mom or Doc is in that position."

He did have a point, much to her relief. "Okay. I'm going to just let it go and not worry about it." She studied Ethan's profile. "Should I be concerned about an old cowboy who's going to do some roping tonight?"

"Yessiree, you need to pray for that cowboy. I've been practicing my roping on some of the cows we've got, and it isn't as easy as it used to be. What happened?"

"You got older."

"Don't remind me," he moaned.

Tessa leaned back against the door. "I think you're going to be fine."

"I hope so." He reached over and covered her hand with his and gave it a squeeze. "I know your cheering will make the difference."

It was a nice thought. She prayed that Doc and her mom would also come to a peace.

The rodeo grounds were located in the southeastern part of Albuquerque. The competition would be held in the Indoor Horse Arena. Next door were the stables and the area for cowboys to camp. The adjacent building housed the concessionaires. Ethan parked his truck and set about unloading Ranger and settling him in the stall assigned by the rodeo authorities. After registering for the calf-roping competition and getting his number, they had close to an hour to kill.

They went to the concessionaire building, and Ethan bought them barbecue sandwiches and bottled tea. The atmosphere of the rodeo reminded Ethan of his teen years, both the good and bad things.

Tessa leaned forward and said, "Would you believe it's been years since I've been to a rodeo?" She laughed and shook her head. "I feel like I'm a rookie again."

"So, you had rodeos in Kentucky?"

"Please. You Westerners don't have a corner on the market. The rest of the country has rodeos."

"Even Kentucky?"

"Kinda. Rodeo competition was becoming popular with the high school kids last time I was there. And the state and local fairs had riding contests. Sometimes they would have demonstrations of roping, but racing in Kentucky is king. Thoroughbreds."

Ethan could understand about the thoroughbreds. "Well, in the West, rodeos are a way of life." He told her about Zach and his experiences growing up. "Zach was on his way to having an all-around belt buckle when he joined the army. He intended on finishing it after he got out. But a roadside bomb changed that."

Tessa squirted more sauce on her sandwich. "He looked fine to me."

"Yeah? You're going to make Zach's day."

She paused and looked at him, waiting for his explanation.

"His right leg is artificial. He lost it after a roadside bomb took out his vehicle. It wasn't until he went to Second-Chance Ranch that he started riding again." He explained the romance that developed between Sophie and Zach.

"Horses are amazing." She looked around at all the cowboys. "I'm looking forward to seeing you calf rope."

Ethan returned her smile. Then the figure entering the refreshment area grabbed his attention and Ethan's expression changed.

"Did I say something wrong?"

His gaze came back to her. "No. I just saw Kevin walk in."

Tessa turned and looked for the man. She found him at the concession stand. "What is he doing here?"

"I don't know."

"I wonder if Mary has served him with the restraining order yet," Tessa commented.

Ethan turned to her. "So Mary got it?"

"Yes." She explained about the delay. "When the judge issued it, Kevin and William were ordered not to come near any of the horses we rescued."

"Good. Why don't we go back and see how Ranger's doing." He glanced at his watch. "It's getting time for me to start saddling Ranger for the competition."

They gathered up their trash and threw it away. Kevin, with his dinner in his hand, stopped in front of Tessa and Ethan.

"Ah, what are you two doing here?" Kevin asked. "Here to watch the competition?"

Smart attitude oozed out of his question, challenging Ethan.

"Ethan is here to compete," Tessa volunteered, pride ringing in her voice.

Her confidence in him settled Ethan's temper.

Kevin's look of surprise was comical.

"What are you here to do?" Ethan asked.

Kevin flushed. He glanced at his date. "C'mon."

They marched off.

"I'd watch him," Ethan said.

Tessa nodded her head. "But for now, let's go see Ranger, because I think you have a date with a horse and a calf."

"And I hope not the dirt."

Tessa sat in the stands, watching the other contestants break out of the chute and go after the calf.

"That was record time of twenty seconds for Scott Avery, from Tucumcari," the announcer broadcast over the PA. "We won't say how old Scott is, but I believe Roosevelt was in office when he graduated."

The crowd laughed. One woman beamed and waved as Scott walked out of the arena.

"Our next contestant is number eighteen, Ethan McClure riding Ranger."

The crowd hushed.

Tessa's stomach tensed. The calf raced out of his chute, and Ethan and Ranger charged out of the next chute. Tessa didn't breathe as Ethan twirled his rope over his head. He threw it and caught the calf around his neck. The rope brought the calf to a halt, landing the cow on its side.

Instantly Ethan was out of the saddle, running to the calf, grabbing his legs and tying them in twenty-two seconds. Tessa was on her feet yelling and clapping with the rest of the crowd.

Ethan stood and walked back to Ranger. The calf struggled, but couldn't get out of the rope. Ethan mounted Ranger and walked his horse forward to relieve pressure on the calf. The arena helpers released the calf and Ethan pulled in his rope.

There were eight others in the competition but at the end of the night, Ethan was number two. The top six contestants of the eighteen were going to compete the next night for the prize.

Hurrying out of the stands, Tessa looked for Ethan inside the building, but didn't see him. She walked over to the next building housing Ranger's stall. There between the rows of stalls was a group of men talking and laughing. Ethan stood in the middle of them. Several of the men patted Ethan on the back. When Ethan saw her, he waved her to his side and introduced her to the group. "Tessa is the new partner in the veterinary practice near us."

Several of the guys stared at her, then looked at Ethan.

"You're funning us, ain't you, Ethan?" Lance Mullen said.

She knew what to expect, so why was she disappointed with Lance's words?

Ethan shook his head. "I wouldn't go there, friend. The lady's got a gift. I've watched her. And if you don't believe me, ask my horse. You know how Ranger won't let anyone near him?"

Lance looked over at Ethan's horse. "Yeah, I found out the hard way."

"The first time I met Dr. Tessa," Ethan informed them, "she was examining Ranger after that bad storm we had several weeks back, and he was as docile as a lamb."

Lance's nose wrinkled in doubt. "Maybe your horse's mellowed."

Ethan folded his arms over his chest. "Try."

Lance looked around and then took up Ethan's challenge and walked to Ranger. The horse's head came up and he danced away. The closer Lance got, the more displeased Ranger became.

"Okay, Lance, that's far enough. Come back here."

Lance joined them.

Ethan grinned at Tessa and nodded his head. She walked to Ranger's side.

"Hello, big boy. How are you?" She rubbed him on his nose. "You did a good job out there tonight."

The horse bobbed his head, accepting the praise.

The crowd of men gawked.

"Can you believe it?" one man croaked.

"Am I seeing things?" another man whispered.

Lance shook his head. "Well, ain't that something."

"She's got you beat," Marv Hanks said, slapping Lance on the back.

Tessa leaned close and kissed Ranger on his nose. "Thanks, big guy, for your help." She rejoined the group.

Several of the guys nodded to her, respect in their eyes. Lance ran his fingers though his hair. "Sorry, ma'am. My mistake."

"That's okay, cowboy. It's nothing I haven't faced before."

"You going to be here for the weekend?" Lance asked, smiling at Tessa.

"Hey, cowboy, back off," Ethan warned. His comment caught the guys by surprise.

Tessa hid her smile of pleasure. Ethan's attitude certainly had changed. "I have to go back to the clinic tonight, but I plan to be back to watch Ethan ride in the finals."

The men said their goodbyes and wandered off.

"I'm proud of you," Ethan told her.

"For what? I'm the one who should be telling you congratulations."

"For handling all those guys so well."

"This isn't my first rodeo, so to speak, and their reaction isn't my first encounter with that attitude."

"Ethan, where are you?"

Tessa and Ethan turned to the voice and saw Beth and Tyler striding toward them.

Beth ran into her brother's arms. "We got here in time to see you rope that calf. Why didn't you let your family know you were competing? And you're in the finals!" She grinned up at her brother. "You could've knocked me over with a sneeze from old Ranger there when I walked into the arena and heard your name called on the PA."

Tyler grinned. "She left me in the dust."

"Well, it shook me up and I wanted to see. I got to the top step and saw you charge out of that chute."

Tyler stepped up and shook Ethan's hand. "Congratulations, old man."

Beth and Tyler turned to see Tessa watching them. "Dr. Grant, it's nice to see you."

"Please call me Tessa."

"So how did you know Ethan was competing tonight?" Beth asked Tessa, a note of mischief in her voice.

Tessa glanced at Ethan, silently questioning him as to what he wanted her to reveal. Before she could say anything else, Ethan spoke. "I asked Tessa here as my date."

Beth's eyes went wide and a satisfied smile curled her mouth. "Oh."

Such a wealth of information was put into that one little word. Her gaze went from Ethan to Tessa. "A date."

"Don't act so shocked," her brother protested.

Beth tried to look innocent but failed.

"What are you doing here, sis?"

"Well, I read in the paper about the old-timers' events and I knew one of the guys who was riding broncos, so we decided to make a night of it. If you'd let me know you were competing, I would've been here in plenty of time."

Tyler leaned down and whispered in her ear, "It was a date."

Beth glanced up at her husband and grinned. "Your point?"

Tyler shook his head.

Beth chatted about the other contestants and Ethan's chances. After several minutes, Ethan said, "I need a favor, sis. Since I didn't count on being in the finals, and I don't want to leave Ranger by himself or pack him up to take him home, would you stay here with Ranger while I take Tessa home?"

"Oh, Ethan, don't impose on them," Tessa protested. "I can—"

"Walk home?" Ethan asked. "There's no taxi service out to the clinic." He paused. "I guess you could drive my truck and bring it back tomorrow."

That thought didn't sit well with Tessa. "I'll call the clinic and have someone pick me up."

Beth waved off the idea. "No, don't do that. We can take Tessa home," Beth cheerfully volunteered. Leaning into her husband, she said, "Can't we?"

"Of course." Tyler hugged his wife's shoulders. "But maybe that's not an option your brother wants."

Beth waved away the thought.

Tessa's choices were limited. Even if she called the clinic, Doc might not be there and she didn't want her mother driving on dark, unfamiliar country roads.

"Thank you, but what about the friend you came to see?" Tessa asked.

"I think he's up next. Let's watch, then we'll drive you home afterward."

They stayed for several more events. After they greeted Beth's friend, Tyler said, "I think we need to get you home, Beth. You've had enough excitement for one night."

Beth took her husband's arm. "I won't break. Pregnant women do all sorts of things."

"True, but I wasn't married to any of the others. Besides, I think Tessa would probably like to get home before midnight."

"Okay." She kissed her brother, took Tyler's arm and started walking away.

"I hope you don't mind?" Ethan said, stepping closer to Tessa.

"Of course I don't mind." She stared at the snaps of his shirt. "You were good out there tonight."

"Who would've thought I could do it? I'll admit, it wasn't as easy as it used to be."

"But you looked impressive."

Ethan looked around and found a concrete ledge running around the inside wall of the building. He grabbed her hand and led her to the ledge. "Up."

"What?"

He urged her to step up and when she did, he bent down and brushed a kiss across her lips. When he drew back, he said, "Thanks for the support."

Her brain wasn't firing right. "For what?"

"For being here."

"I'm glad you asked me." She glanced over his shoulder to see Beth grinning. "We have an audience."

He shrugged. "I know, but I wanted to kiss you, and if I bent over...well, my back appreciates you being up on the ledge."

Her brow arched. "Not as young as you used to be?"

"True. I'll need the liniment I brought for Ranger." He ran his hand through his hair. "This is not the way I planned to end our date."

"No?"

"No. I wasn't counting on my sister driving you home afterward."

"We'll just say 'to be continued tomorrow night,' won't we?"

He helped her down from the ledge. "I like your thinking."

Beth stood waiting, a big grin on her face.

"My ride awaits. Good night, Ethan."

As she walked out of the corral area to join Beth and Tyler, she felt Ethan's gaze on her and remembered his unexpected kiss. She should be embarrassed Beth witnessed it, but somehow she wasn't.

Ethan walked back to his horse trailer parked at the end of the row where Ranger was housed. The front of the horse trailer had a small compartment equipped with a bunk, small closet and dresser. Ranger's bridle and saddle were in the closet, and Ethan's things in the dresser.

As Ethan shucked off his boots, his mind went to Tessa. He'd spotted her in the crowd before Ranger had burst out of the chute after the steer. Knowing she was out there settled him. He couldn't explain it, but he felt they were establishing a bond that could lead to deeper things.

Tessa was an amazing woman, with her determination to become a vet—and from what he'd seen, a good one.

It didn't matter that she had to stand on a stool for him to kiss her, it was worth the effort. He'd never had these feelings before. Taking off his shirt and belt, he stretched out on the bunk. Folding his arms behind his head, he prayed for God's direction.

The last thing he remembered before drifting off to sleep was the image of Tessa sitting in Lady's stall, asleep.

"Ethan competing tonight surprised me," Beth commented. "And what was more of a surprise was he didn't let his family know."

Tyler, Beth and Tessa were cramped into the front seat of Tyler's truck. Tessa got the feeling that Beth wasn't surprised at her brother's choice to bring her to the rodeo, but not telling his siblings about the competition.

"I was surprised when he told me what he was going to do," Tessa replied, hoping to defuse the situation.

"He quit competing his senior year in high school. It was a mystery to us all why Ethan walked away from rodeoing. Now suddenly he wants to compete. I don't understand."

Tyler reached over and patted Beth's leg. "Quit trying to figure out your brother's motives. He's a grown man and entitled to do what he wants."

Beth wrapped her hand around her husband's arm and rested her head on his shoulder. "I know, but I just find it curious that he's acting so strange." She glanced at Tessa, a calculated look in her eyes.

"I'm sure he has his reasons," Tessa offered.

"True, but I'm just trying to understand," Beth replied.

Tessa recognized a sister's probing when she saw it. "I can't claim I understand everything he did tonight, either. For one thing, he didn't tell me he was bringing his horse on the date."

Tyler snorted and Beth's eyes widened, then

she laughed. "Well, he's kinda rusty," Beth added.

"Ya think?" Tessa grinned, and immediately Beth's expression changed and Tessa knew she'd won an ally. "I guess I was being naive. If he was going to compete, he needed his horse."

"I'll give it to my brother, he's the only guy I know who'd take his horse on a date."

Tessa laughed and Beth joined.

"I guess if you're going to ask a vet out, it isn't beyond the realm of possibility."

The women laughed harder.

When she could talk again, Beth added, "You know, he's a very special guy. Rusty, but special."

Tessa knew exactly what Beth was saying. It touched her heart that Beth was protective of her older brother. In the light from the dash's lights, Tessa looked Beth in the eye. "I do know."

Beth searched Tessa's face, and Tessa knew Beth was weighing and evaluating her. Apparently, Beth approved, because she nodded her consent.

They pulled into the clinic's parking lot.

"Thank you for the ride." Tessa opened the door and nodded to Tyler and Beth.

"We'll see you tomorrow night," Beth called out.

"See you then."

Tessa opened the screen door on the breezeway and tried the back door. It was unlocked. The lights in the kitchen were on, but the rest of the house was dark. Her mom sat at the table, a mug in her hand. When she looked up, there was a world of confusion and hurt in her eyes before the mask went back up.

"What's wrong, Mom?"

"Nothing. What makes you think anything is wrong?"

"You're up, drinking coffee at this hour."

Tessa put her purse down on the table.

"The phone rang and Doc Adams answered it. He went into the clinic. That was several minutes ago."

Tessa walked into the clinic and found Doc packing his medical bag. "What's the emergency?"

"The Barlows. The rescue horse at their

ranch. He was fine earlier in the evening, but now he's down rolling. I've got to get there."

"Do you want me to go?" Tessa asked.

"No. I can do it." He walked into the kitchen and pulled his keys off the hook inside the back door. Tessa followed him.

"Are you sure I can't help? I mean, wasn't that one of the reasons you hired me?"

"It is, but since your mom's here, I want you to be able to spend time with her." He glanced at Joan who sat at the table staring at her coffee before turning back to Tessa. "So how was your date? I didn't hear Ethan."

"That's because Beth and Tyler brought me home."

Doc paused. "Oh, I hope that isn't a bad sign."

"No, it's a good sign. Ethan is one of the finalists in the calf-roping competition and needed to stay in Albuquerque. He offered to drive me home, but his sister and brother-in-law were there so they volunteered to bring me."

Doc nodded. "I'm glad for Ethan. I'll contact you if I need any help."

Tessa watched Doc get in his truck. She slowly turned around and faced her mother.

"I'm surprised you're drinking coffee this late."

Joan looked up from the mug. "I couldn't sleep." One shoulder lifted. "And there was coffee on the stove."

Her mother couldn't sleep and she drank coffee? That didn't make sense.

"So, you had a good time?" Joan seemed to come out of her "mood" and turned her attention on Tessa.

"I had fun." Tessa sat across from her mother at the table. "Watching Ethan was, well, it was amazing."

"Oh?" Her mother's all-seeing gaze rested on her.

"Before the event, we ate sandwiches in the refreshment area, and I couldn't have enjoyed myself more if we'd gone to a four-star restaurant, which we did for the board meeting." Tessa thought about their laughing and the pure joy of the moment. "He's special, Mom."

Reaching out, Joan clasped her daughter's hand. "I'm glad. I've been worried that you buried yourself in your schooling, ignoring all the boys who were interested in you after that rotten engagement." Releasing Tessa's hand, Joan wrapped her hands around her mug.

"At first, I was glad you didn't give up your career for 'that man' who wanted a ticket through law school." She closed her eyes. "I wanted you to finish school and have a career so you could always support yourself. But afterward—"

Leaning forward, Tessa whispered, "It's not been that long. Some of the girls I graduated with from high school are still single."

Joan waved that point off. "I know." Joan sighed. "But there were other guys who were interested in you and didn't need a meal ticket."

"Mom, you encouraged me to finish my education above all else. I wanted that, too." The unspoken thought between them was that neither of them wanted Tessa to be in the position of marrying straight out of high school and ending up with a man who drank and gambled.

The clock in the kitchen chimed eleven.

"You're right. I did want you to have your

degree, but I also want you to be happy. And that's why I'm excited that you like Ethan."

Tessa opened her mouth to respond, but her mom continued to talk.

"When that special man walks into your life, it's like nothing you've ever experienced. You just know."

"Really?"

Joan's eyes took on a faraway look as she remembered her own love. "It doesn't matter what age you are, when *that* man shows up, your heart kicks into overdrive and you just want to spend time with him. You think about him and can't wait to talk to him again. Just walking out with him, hand in hand in the park, is a wonderful experience."

Tessa stared at her mother. She'd never heard her mom talk like that about her father. "Is that how you felt about dad?"

The question jerked Joan out of her musings. "It was." She stood and walked to the sink and emptied her coffee mug into it. "I'm going to bed. I'm glad you had a good time, sweetheart. It's time."

Tessa sat at the table and thought about what

her mother had said. From what she could re-member, there had always been a strain be-tween her parents, which made her nervous about how her relationship with Ethan would fare.

The memories took the joy out of her eve-ning.

Chapter Ten

Tessa got up early to fix breakfast for everyone. When she glanced outside, Doc's truck still hadn't returned. She located the Barlows' phone number and called.

"They're finishing up now," Connie Barlow explained. "Doc was able to pull the horse through, but it took work. I'll feed Doc breakfast before he leaves."

"Thanks, Connie."

Doc arrived back at the clinic a little after nine. From his expression, the night's work had exhausted him.

"I'm glad you were able to save the horse," Tessa told him as she poured him a cup of coffee.

"Thanks." He settled in a chair and took a sip of the coffee. Joan sat watching them.

After he took several sips, he shook his head. "That horse was poisoned."

"What?" both women exclaimed.

"The hay in the horse's stall was tainted. Oddly, we didn't find any other contaminated hay anywhere else in the stables."

"Only in the rescue horse's stall?" Tessa asked.

"Only there."

"Did Steve have any explanation?" Joan asked.

"No, he didn't. But I know Steve Barlow. He wouldn't feed any horse bad hay."

Tessa sat at the table with her mom and Doc. "How could that hay only be in that one horse's stall?"

Doc sighed. "I've seen this before. When Doris had an argument with one of her neighbors several years ago, his stock ended up being poisoned. No one could prove Doris had anything to do with it, but she seemed pleased with what happened."

Joan's eyes widened. "This Doris person would do something like that?"

"I'm afraid so. She wasn't happy her horses were taken from her."

"Have you notified the sheriff?" Tessa asked. "You know the court issued that restraining order against William and Kevin."

"Steve was going to call him. I'll need to put out the word to the other people caring for those rescued horses about what happened. They'll need to be on guard."

"And tell everyone you talk to about the restraining order. I'll call Mary, and let her know about this development." Tessa remembered when Kevin showed up at the clinic wanting his horse. "We'll need to keep extra watch on Lady and Hope."

Doc pushed away the coffee cup. "If you don't mind, I'm going to hit the sheets for a couple of hours of shut-eye. I'll leave everything in your capable hands, Dr. Tessa." He stood and disappeared down the hall.

Dr. Tessa. She liked how that sounded and hoped others would start calling her that.

Joan turned to her daughter. "You need any help with the animals in the clinic?"

It touched Tessa that her mom offered to help. "It's been a while since you worked in a barn."

"True, but I think things will come back to me."

"Sure, if that's what you want."

"It is."

"Let me contact Mary and tell her what happened, then we can go into the barn and work."

After the call, arm in arm, they walked into the stables, reminding Tessa of one of the good memories she had from her childhood of all three of them working together in the barn. They were among her very few good memories.

The day passed swiftly for Tessa and her mom. They went on one call together and when they got back, Doc was up. Anticipation built for Tessa throughout the day. When she got ready to leave at five, her mother and Doc were in the kitchen waiting.

"I thought it might be nice to see Ethan

ride," Doc said. "I think Joan would like to see it, too."

The shock and surprise must've shown clearly on Tessa's face because her mother hastily added, "If we go with you, besides seeing Ethan, we can drive your truck back to the clinic and you could ride home with Ethan."

And his horse, Tessa silently added. The looks on their faces told Tessa that Doc and her mom didn't want to spend another night alone together. "Okay. I think that might work out."

Doc's shoulders sagged and her mother sighed in relief. What was the matter with them?

"Since I'm going to drive," Doc began, "why don't we take my truck?"

"You don't want to take Tessa's new truck?" Joan asked.

Doc froze.

"Mom, let's take Doc's truck. If anything happens at the rodeo, he'll have his supplies."

"Oh, that's a good idea."

Tessa caught Doc's nod of thanks, but there was something else in his eyes she couldn't identify.

* * *

Ethan couldn't wait to see Tessa tonight. Hopefully, the second half of the date would turn out better than the first. As Ethan was checking out Ranger's hooves to make sure he hadn't picked up anything, he heard his parents' voices. When he looked up, he saw his mom and dad accompanied by his sister and her husband barreling down the aisle. Trailing behind were Zach and Sophie.

Ethan stood.

"Son, we're here to lend you our support," Lynda announced as she came to his side. He'd told his parents he was coming to the rodeo, and might stay overnight, but he hadn't wanted to tell them he was going to try to compete in case he ended up eating dirt. He glared at his sister.

She shrugged. "When Mom called this morning and asked if I saw you last night, I told her yes and that you finaled in calf roping."

Lynda kissed her son's cheek, then gave him a stern look. "Imagine having to find out from your youngest child that your oldest son was a finalist in the calf roping? I'm lucky one of the ladies in my Bible study didn't call and ask about you competing."

"Mom, it's the old-timers' competition," Ethan defended himself. "Not something to brag about."

From her expression, his mother wasn't buying.

Zach stepped up and said, "I think if he did a face-plant, Mom, he wouldn't want witnesses—particularly his mother."

"Zach," his mom chided.

"What?" he asked innocently.

Lynda ignored him and turned back to Ethan. "You're forgiven for not telling your mother, but even if you hadn't made the finals, I would've wanted to see you."

Recognizing his mother's chastening, he nodded. "Thanks, Mom, for the support." Glancing over his mother's shoulder, he saw his dad grinning from ear to ear.

"Can we join the party?" Doc Adams asked, stopping by Lynda. Tessa and her mother stood beside Doc.

Ethan caught Tessa's gaze, silently asking

what had happened. She shrugged and nodded toward his family. He could only shake his head. So much for their date.

"Please, join us," Ken McClure spoke. "Are you here to see Ethan?"

"She is," Beth volunteered. "She was here last night and watched Ethan."

All the McClures turned toward Ethan. His mother's brow arched.

"We had a date," Ethan explained.

Looks were traded. Color rose in Tessa's cheeks.

Feeling like a bug under glass, Ethan wanted to talk to Tessa privately. "You might want to go get seats in the stands before it fills up. The roping contest is going to start in about a half hour."

His family said their goodbyes. As they drifted off, Ethan stepped to Tessa's side. "Let's walk."

She nodded. Once they were away from family and friends, Ethan said, "I'm sorry about the crowd. I wasn't expecting them."

"That's okay. I brought my own crowd. I think none of us were comfortable leaving my mom and Doc to themselves tonight." She rubbed her arms. "There was a lot of tension in the house when I got back to the clinic last night. They wanted to come tonight and I thought—if I rode here with them, I could ride back with you."

His eyes twinkled. "I like your thinking."

"And I wanted to tell you, if someone hasn't already told you, one of the rescue horses was given tainted hay. Doc went out to the Barlows' place last night and they were able to counteract the poison, but that hay was found nowhere else at their place."

"A deliberate act."

She nodded. "We think so. Steve's alerted the sheriff about what happened." She paused and looked up at him. "I think all the families housing the rescued horses need to be put on alert. I notified Mary of the poisoning, too."

"Good." Something was going on here beyond just a grudge for Doris and William.

"Mom and I checked Lady's and Hope's hay. Everything looks kosher."

"That's a smart idea." He paused, then asked, "Your mother worked out at the stables?"

"Yes. It might've been several years since she's worked at feeding stock, but she still knows her way around and was a big help while Doc was sleeping. He was up all night with that horse at the Barlows' place."

"I think Doc picked a winner when he got you." The approval in his eyes echoed what he said.

She blushed. "How'd things go around here today?"

"I had a few nostalgic memories." He shrugged. "Saw friends from years ago." And had some nightmares come back to him that he wished he'd forgotten. He'd learned lessons that he'd been sharing with others for a while now. "I'm glad you're here now." He grabbed her hand and gave it a squeeze. "Ranger's been interested in all the activity."

"You have a nosy horse?"

"C'mon, Tessa, you know horses are curious."

"Only if they are as well fed and cared for as Ranger is. I will say that Lady had started showing signs of her personality. Today, Mom was in her stall and Lady didn't like how Mom was arranging the hay and head-butted Mom. I laughed so hard and then kissed Lady on her nose. I think when Lady's completely recovered she'll make her wishes known. She'll be a wonderful horse for some family. And Hope is full of life and joy. She's a lively filly."

Tessa smiled at him and Ethan felt his heart turn over. They shared a special bond over Hope. "That's good to know."

The announcer came on the loudspeaker, announcing the next event, calf roping.

"That's my signal. I'll look for you in the stands."

"Good luck, Ethan." Tessa crooked her finger for him to bend down. When he did, she brushed a kiss across his lips.

"That's for good luck."

He felt the goofy expression come over his face. "Thanks."

Straightening up, he nodded and headed toward Ranger to saddle him for the competition. No matter what happened, he felt he'd won.

* * *

As Tessa stood watching Ethan saddle Ranger, a voice whispered in her ear, "That was touching."

Turning, she came face-to-face with Kevin. "Are you here to watch the competition?"

The smile Kevin flashed her made her skin crawl. "I'm here to watch and observe."

Something inside of her urged her to walk away. "Have a good night." She walked past him to get to the stands. His hand shot out, stopping her.

"I still want my horse," Kevin told her, all friendliness wiped from his face.

She looked down at his hand, then up at him. He released her arm. "You need to take up your grievance with the court, Mr. Raney. I have no say."

Before he could answer, they heard, "There he is."

They looked around and a tall, solid man walked up to Kevin and handed him a folded sheet of paper. "Kevin Raney, you've been served." The man turned around and walked by the woman who'd ID'd Kevin. She pocketed some money.

Kevin looked at the restraining order. "What's this?" He opened the folded piece of paper. From his fierce expression, Tessa guessed the restraining order the Society swore out had been served.

His face darkened with rage. "Are you behind this?"

"No. But I think the ranchers you've been visiting are behind it since you keep showing up wherever the Society has the rescue horses. The court has forbidden you from going near those ranchers."

The muscles in his jaw flexed. "Don't think this will stop me."

She didn't answer him, but walked away from the man, her insides trembling.

She hurried into the arena and searched for her family and Ethan's in the stands. Sophie saw Tessa and waved her to where they all were sitting. Tessa waved back and started toward them.

On her way to where the family sat, Tessa spotted Mary. Tessa made a slight detour and sat next to Mary. The man next to her had his arm around Mary's shoulders.

"Tessa." Mary drew back in surprise. She glanced at Ethan's family, then back at Tessa. "What are you doing here and not over there?"

"A minute ago, the process server found Kevin and gave him the restraining order. He wasn't happy."

"You saw that?"

"He was talking—well, needling—me when it happened."

Mary sighed. "I knew he wouldn't be happy. Let's just send out emails to the ranchers warning them."

Sounded good to Tessa. "I just wanted you to know."

"Thanks for the heads-up."

Tessa nodded and started toward her and Ethan's families. Hearing the announcer, she hurried to Lynda McClure's side.

Ethan's family looked at her and Tessa saw questions in their eyes. Tessa explained about the incident with Kevin.

"We'll be on the lookout," Ken said.

After watching the first three finalists,

Lynda sighed. "When is it going to be Ethan's turn?"

"He'll be the next to the last," Ken told her.

"He was great last night, Mom," Beth assured them. "Have you seen him practicing?"

Lynda looked at her husband. "No, have you, Ken?"

Ken opened his mouth, then paused. "He's spent some time out in the pasture where there are a few head of cattle." He shook his head. "I wondered why he was riding out so often."

The question was dropped when the announcer introduced the next rider. Over the next half hour the other finalists rode and roped. Finally, the only two finalists left, Ethan and the top finalist.

"Next up, ladies and gentlemen, is Ethan McClure from the Bar-M ranch, riding his horse, Ranger."

Tessa held her breath as the horn sounded and the calf raced out of the chute. Ethan and Ranger charged after the calf and Ethan threw his rope. The calf was jerked off his feet and Ethan anchored the rope to the saddled horn. He jumped off Ranger and had the rope around the calf's legs in record time. He stood and waited for the calf to try to undo the bindings. The calf struggled to stand and the rope came undone.

The disqualifying buzzer sounded. And the announcer came on and said, "It was the fastest time so far, 17.2 seconds. And if that calf had stayed down, Ethan would be in first place."

Ethan shook his head, but the crowd stood and clapped for him. He acknowledged the crowd and rewound his rope.

His family, Tessa, Joan and Doc filed out of the stands, and walked back to the stall where Ranger had been housed. When Ethan came back to the stall, he was walking his horse.

His family hugged him and told him they were proud of him. Doc and Joan added their praise and sympathy.

"You were faster tonight, Ethan, than you were last night," Tessa said.

"I was, but the rope didn't hold." He shrugged. "That's the breaks."

"No matter. I'm proud of you, son," Ken McClure told Ethan. "Now I know why you were spending so much time out in the north pasture. I couldn't figure out what was so interesting out there. I wondered if you were digging a trench."

Snickers and choked laughter filled the air.

Ethan grinned. "This was something I wanted to try, but needed to know I wouldn't fall on my face in front of everyone. I did some practicing."

"And now I understand all those hot baths you were taking. I couldn't figure out why my son suddenly decided to hog the tub," Lynda added.

After the laughter died down and Ethan received more congratulations, the group got ready to leave.

"You're going to ride home with me, aren't you?" Ethan asked Tessa loud enough that everyone heard.

"I am."

Ethan turned to his family. "Thanks for the support."

Ken leaned over and whispered in his son's ear.

"You have the truck?"

His father smiled.

"Thanks, Dad."

Ethan turned back to Tessa. "This time, our date will end a little differently. I'll take you home and we won't have to worry about Ranger chaperoning us. Dad's taking him home."

Beth gave her father a thumbs-up. "Good call, Dad."

Ethan's father's support slid into Tessa's heart. She smiled her thanks. Ken nodded. When Tessa looked at Lynda, her attitude mirrored her husband's.

That approval appeared on Ethan's brother's and sister's faces, too. How very comforting to be certain of his family's acceptance of her.

Ken shot into action packing up Ranger and hooking up the trailer.

Doc and Joan said goodbye and left.

When Ken drove away with Ranger's trailer in tow, Ethan turned to Tessa.

"Would you like to go to the Dairy Mart and get an ice cream?"

"You noticed that I love their ice cream?"

"I do notice other things beside horses and

cows." He grinned, finding a path straight into her heart.

"Sounds like a winner."

Chapter Eleven

Tessa sat across from Ethan in one of the booths at the local Dairy Mart drive-in. She had a soft-serve ice cream cone, while Ethan devoured a banana split.

Ethan felt Tessa's eyes on him. He took that last bite of his treat and placed the spoon in the plastic dish. "That was good." He leaned back and grinned at her. "That's the first banana split I've had in years."

"You're on a roll, aren't you? You've competed in the rodeo and now you've had a banana split."

He could've added falling in love to the list. "I just decided to push myself."

Tilting her head to the right, she studied him.

"You said you stopped doing rodeo your senior year. Why?"

He hadn't anticipated the question. What could he tell her? "When I was in high school the ranch went through a bad time. There was a drought, the stock had to be fed with bought hay and we just didn't have any extra money. My parents couldn't afford to keep two of us competing in rodeo. Zach was rated higher than I, so it was decided he should continue."

She opened her mouth, but he held up his hand. "I suggested it. I got a partial scholarship to college, but there was no extra money for rodeo, especially if you didn't place." There was another reason why he didn't compete between graduating from high school and college, but he knew that Tessa wouldn't understand.

Tessa's expression softened. "I know exactly what you're talking about. My mom couldn't afford to pay for me to go to college after my dad disappeared. So I worked hard in high school and won a scholarship."

He breathed a sigh of relief that she understood. "You ready?"

She popped the last bite of her ice cream into her mouth. "I am." She grinned at him. "I must admit, you've taken me some places I haven't been in a long time."

"Are you saying I'm cheap?" he asked as they walked out of the Dairy Mart.

"No. I'd say you're creative in your choices of restaurants."

"Do I get points for creativity?"

"You do."

"Okay, okay. I owe you a nice dinner. But does that mean the church dinner next Friday night is out?"

"Okay, you get that one." Her laughter and smile wrapped themselves around his heart, fanning feelings as exciting as they were new.

They laughed and talked as they drove back to the clinic, swapping stories about horses, stock and animal rescues. She understood the things going on at the ranch and the problems they had with the Rescue Society.

"So how is it going? Do you like New Mexico?"

"Love it, but it takes some getting used to." She shook her head and grinned. "You know,

I thought Doc didn't know what he was talking about with the GPS, but he nailed it. So the day when I forgot the map he gave me— and that was accidental—I ended up driving around for hours trying to find my way with no signal. I had to eat some crow."

"You're not the first one. I've really pulled some boneheaded stunts, myself."

"Oh, want to share?"

"I think I'd hold those in reserve. I don't want to scare you off."

Her brow arched.

"I hope you didn't mind all my family showing up tonight."

Her smile eased his tension. "Nice divert."

They glanced at each other and laughed. He reached over, grabbed her hand and squeezed it. He just couldn't believe that God had dropped this wonderful woman into his midst. How perfect were they for each other?

He turned into the graveled parking lot of the clinic and stopped. He hurried around the truck to open her door.

She slipped her arm through his and walked

with him to the breezeway screen door. As he bent down to kiss her, he heard angry voices.

Tessa heard them too.

They both thought the same thing—trouble with Doris and William over the rescued horses. They charged into the walkway and opened the kitchen door.

"You should've told me, Joan. You didn't have the right to keep that secret," Doc yelled, his voice coming from the living room.

"If I'd told you, Vince, what would you have done?"

"I would've quit school and married you. You knew I loved you."

"Then what? Work at the local pet store for minimum wage?"

"We would've made it," he came back. "But you took that decision away from me."

"I loved you too much to take your dream away from you," Joan answered, her voice quivering.

"Instead you robbed me of my child? An incredible woman who loves horses as much as I do."

"You don't understand," Joan sobbed. She

ran down the hall past the kitchen. When she saw Tessa and Ethan just inside the back door, she froze.

Doc raced after her, stopping short when he saw who stood in the kitchen.

Tessa stood shock-still. Both Doc and Joan looked at Tessa's stricken expression.

"Tessa," her mother breathed.

As if coming out of a stupor, Tessa stepped forward. "What were you two talking about? Did you know each other before you married Dad?"

Doc and Joan traded stricken looks, guilt coloring their expressions.

"I need to explain," Joan started.

Tessa looked so brittle that Ethan was afraid she'd break. He put his hand on her shoulder and quietly said, "I think it might help if you sat down."

Doc and Joan agreed and walked to the table. Ethan guided Tessa to a chair and held it for her. Once seated, he said, "I'll go and leave you all to talk."

Tessa grasped his arm, manacling him to

her side. "No." She looked up at him. "Please stay."

Glancing at the other two, they nodded. Ethan thought he saw relief in Doc's eyes.

Sitting, Ethan took Tessa's hand in his. They all looked at Joan.

Licking her lips, Joan took a deep breath. "As I told you before, Tessa, between my junior and senior years in high school, one summer night, my friends and I went to the local drive-in. There was this cute short-order cook who'd just started working there. When I looked in the window, I saw him and he smiled at me. My heart nearly burst out of my chest." The memory caused Joan to smile. "One of the car-hops was a friend of mine, and I asked her about him." Joan glanced at Doc and her expression softened.

Ethan felt Tessa's hand tighten.

Joan turned back to her daughter. "Well, I met the boy when he got off work. But he didn't have a lot of time, because he needed to get home. He had another job at one of the local veterinary's clinics that started at five in the morning. He worked there days and at the burger joint at night. But he still took the time to walk me home.

"I found out the reason he was working two jobs was to get enough money to finish his last semester of college."

Tessa's brow wrinkled in a frown. "His last semester?"

Doc finally spoke. "I ran out of money half-way through my senior year and had to take a semester off and work to earn enough money. It took me four and half years to finish my degree."

"Go on," Tessa encouraged.

Clearing her throat, Joan resumed her story. "His goal was to become a vet. He was from a poor family in the hills of Kentucky, but he had a dream of working with animals. He loved animals."

That hadn't changed in Doc, Ethan knew. The man had a way with animals, much like Tessa.

"We fell in love that summer, despite him working all that time. I helped out at the clinic and spent all my money at the drive-in." Joan stared at her hands. "He went back to school in the fall and we wrote. He'd told me he applied for a scholarship to go to veterinary school at Purdue. He graduated from college and won the scholarship." Joan's voice fell to a whisper. "The day I got Vince's letter telling me he got the scholarship was the day I discovered I was pregnant." When she looked up, her eyes found Doc's face. There was pain there.

"I couldn't hide it long from my parents. They guessed Vince was the father. My dad was not an understanding man. He threw me out of the house. My mom didn't stand up to him. She never did.

"I went to live with my grandmother in Mount Sterling. I told her I wanted to keep my baby. She sided with me against my dad and protected me from his wrath. She couldn't understand how her daughter, my mother, would allow any man to rule her like Dad did."

Doc rested his hand over Joan's. She didn't look at him, but stared at his hand.

"I tried to find Joan at Christmas," Doc added. "Her parents said she was gone, but would never say where. I asked Joan's friends, but no one was talking. I didn't know why everyone looked at me like I had the plague." Doc shook his head. "I don't know why I was that stupid."

Joan raised her head and looked in amazement at the man.

"I checked several times with Joan's parents and got the same response. The last time, the Christmas after I started veterinary school, her father greeted me with a shotgun and told me never to come to his house again or I'd regret it."

"Sounds like my dad." Joan didn't look at Doc but grabbed a tablet kept on the table for note taking if an emergency was called in, and started to fiddle with it.

Tessa's gaze went back to her mother. Ethan could see her struggling to understand the truths that had come to light in the last few minutes. "So how did you come to marry D— Warren?"

Joan didn't meet anyone's eyes, but stared down at the table. "I was working at one of the hardware stores near my grandmother's house, when Warren came in to buy chicken wire for his ranch. We struck up a conversation. Over the next two months, we became friends. He was a sea of calm in my storm. It was obvious what my condition was, but he didn't pass judgment. One day he proposed. Shocked me speechless. I liked him, but didn't love him and he knew it. He also knew that my dad had thrown me out. I told him I wasn't ready to start another relationship. He accepted my explanation but left the proposal open.

"I thought about it. I thought about trying to raise you as a single mother, without even a high school diploma. I reasoned that most marriages a hundred years ago were practical, based on making life easier. I thought I could grow to love him. He thought so, too.

"It never happened." Her fingers folded a corner of the top sheet on the pad of paper.

They waited for Joan to continue. The tension in the room notched up.

Listening to Joan talk about marrying a friend, Ethan realized how he'd dodged a bullet when Mary had stood him up.

"So instead of marrying the man you loved," Tessa threw out, "you married a man who drank away our lives and made our lives miserable."

Joan gasped. The shock in Doc's eyes held Ethan still.

"Tessa," Joan began.

"Don't, Mom. Don't sugarcoat it. Instead of marrying the man you loved, you married a man who turned into a miserable drunk who spent his time either yelling or drinking himself into a stupor. Growing up, I was too afraid to ask anyone to the house, fearing that Dad would be drunk, and I wouldn't know which drunk would appear. The happy, sloppy drunk, or the mean, bitter drunk who screamed all the time."

Joan's stricken expression broke Ethan's heart. Doc looked shell-shocked.

In her anger, Tessa seemed oblivious to anyone's reaction, caught in her own world. "Remember when he started disappearing for days on end? We didn't know where he was or if he would come home. The tension was worse then, Mom, not knowing. That was until the day when the sheriff showed up at the door with an eviction notice." Tessa jerked to her feet, causing the chair to tip backward. It crashed to the floor, causing Joan to jump, but Tessa was unaware, caught in her storm of anger and hurt. "No, marrying a drunken gambler was the better way," Tessa spat out and raced out of the kitchen.

The dead silence pressed in on the three people left behind.

"I didn't know," came Joan's choked words. "I didn't know how she felt. I should've, but…" She rose to go after Tessa, but Doc grabbed her arm, stopping her. He stood, facing her.

"I have to talk to her, Vince." Tears ran down Joan's face as she tried to get out of Doc's grasp.

"Later, Joannie. Not now. She's not ready to hear anything you or I have to say."

"Oh, my poor baby." The words came from her gut. The woman collapsed into herself.

Doc drew Joan into his arms and held her while she came apart. He looked over his shoulder at Ethan. Doc nodded toward the barn.

Ethan doubted the wisdom of trying to talk to Tessa just now, not after the hurt and anger that flowed out of her. But even if she wasn't ready to talk, he could hold her and pray for her. For only Heaven could touch her heart right now.

Tessa stumbled into an empty stall in the corner of the stables. Suddenly, the strength in her legs vanished and she collapsed into a heap on the hay.

"Oh, God." The tears finally overwhelmed her and she turned her face into the hay. The storm washed over her—the grief, agony and pain of living with a gambler and drunk. She cried for all the missed dates, the loneliness, the fear that she'd held at bay during the years Warren was with them.

The tides of unhappiness kept coming in waves. She tried to catch her breath, but another wave would swamp her. Finally, after what seemed hours, there appeared an island of calm in the midst of her storm.

She could see it and struggled toward it. Finally, the storm abated, and when she could feel something beside the ache and betrayal, she heard the steady beat of a heart. Then she became aware of the warmth surrounding her. And the gentle stroking of a large hand on her back.

She opened her eyes, or tried to. They were swollen, but she could see Ethan's shirt under her cheek.

He tipped up her chin and kissed her forehead.

He didn't try to say anything, try to make explanations, but simply held her.

She didn't want to think. She just wanted to rest in a moment of peace.

After several minutes, Ethan said, "That's why Doc never married."

She looked up at him. "What?"

"We always wondered why Doc didn't marry. There were several eligible ladies and widows around here who showed interest. He was social, went to parties, but always kept things with those ladies very low key.

"My sister, Beth, used to spin stories about how she thought his heart might've been—"

She jerked out of his hold.

Ethan didn't say anything, but she saw his embarrassment.

"—broken?" Tessa supplied. "Well, maybe the stories your sister came up with were closer to the truth than she knew."

"Maybe."

"And won't your sister be surprised to learn her speculation was right?"

He studied her. "I don't know how she's gonna find out."

Tessa gave a bark of laughter. "It's not a secret that will stay hidden much longer."

"Tessa, I'm not going to say anything. No one has to know."

Struggling to her feet, a harsh laugh escaped Tessa. Now that the grief and hurt had passed, the void inside of her filled with another emotion—anger. "No? How are you going to look at Doc, now? Or me? I'm his daughter." She stood there and the color drained from her face. "I'm his daughter," came the whispered words. "He would've been such a wonderful father."

"I think you're right."

"Instead, we lived with a man who was a Jekyll & Hyde."

Ethan got to his feet. "I'm sure your mother meant well."

She turned on him. "You don't understand the terror and inconsistency we lived with. My dad—Warren—gambled. Who knows why, but when he started losing, he started drinking. I remember one Christmas in particular. I'd just turned ten. The day after, men showed up at our front door and took my new bicycle with them. And the new blender my mom got. They both were payment for gambling debts Warren owed."

Ethan winced.

The more she thought about it, the angrier she became.

"I remember when the men took those presents away, I was so glad that we lived out in the country where we had no neighbors to see. And when I went to school after Christmas vacation, everyone bragged about their presents and showed them off. When they asked me what I got, what could I say? If I said a bike, my schoolmates would wonder where it was.

"That wasn't the only time it happened. It got to the point where if a stranger drove up to the house, we didn't know if he was going to haul something off or yell at us about money for gambling debts.

"And do you know what, Ethan? I never blamed my mom for a single moment for the situation, because we shared it. Because I thought the man was my father.

"Not now." With those words ringing through the stillness of the stable, she walked out of the stable into the night. She didn't want the anger vibrating through her to spill over onto him.

Ethan didn't come after her as she walked out into the night.

The kitchen stood empty when Ethan came back into the house. "Doc?"

Doc walked out of the living room. He looked like the walking wounded. "How's Tessa?"

"She's not taking it well."

"Understandable." Doc collapsed into one of the kitchen chairs. "I don't believe it." Shaking his head, he said, "I nearly passed out when Joan showed up at the clinic door, looking for

Tessa. When I could talk again, I asked why she wanted to see her. When she told me she was Tessa's mom, my mind couldn't take it in. I felt like I was living in some alternate universe. Before I could question Joan more, you brought Tessa home.

"Last night, when you two went on your date, I vowed I wouldn't pry into Joan's life. It never occurred to me…"

Ethan wanted to say something to help Doc, but what words could he say?

"Then I started thinking about something you said to me, about how Tessa gentled a horse like I do, that we approached the animals with the same attitude. First time I saw her do that, I thought to myself how fortunate I was Tessa came. I kept thinking about her natural ability to calm animals. And the more I looked at the way Tessa did things, the more I recognized myself in her. I just thought it a freak accident—that maybe all good vets did it that way. Then Joan showed up." He fell silent. "And I started wondering. And tonight—

"I had a family all this time and didn't know," Doc's choked whisper came. Looking up, he smiled sadly at Ethan. "You and your family were the closest thing I had. I always consider myself your favorite uncle. I was a guide in addition to your father."

"You were," Ethan reassured him, leaning forward on his elbows. "You were the one I could turn to when I got in trouble. You helped but made me pay for my mistakes." He sat back. "I guess I know now why you remained single."

"When I was growing up in those mountains of Kentucky, I knew we were poor, but it really didn't matter. But when I got to high school, and knew I wanted to be a vet, I searched and searched around for a way to go to school. I had an English teacher who came from Vermont and she knew what I wanted to do. She pointed me in the right direction.

"It took sweat and blood to earn the grades to win a scholarship. My dad thought it was nonsense, but mother wanted more for me. Of course, I was the fifth of seven children and there was no money to spare."

"But you made it."

"I did. Getting the degree was the most important thing in my life until the summer I met Joan. I loved her from the first instant I saw her." Doc smiled. Ethan guessed he was reliving that summer.

"She was four years younger, but that didn't matter to us. When she disappeared, it just never occurred to me she was pregnant." The pain in Doc's eyes made Ethan squirm. "I just thought that she maybe met some young man and ran off. I knew there was the son of one of the wealthy horse owners in the area that liked Joan. I saw him hanging around her. I just assumed that maybe in the end she wanted a wealthy man instead of a poor kid from the hills."

"I guess you didn't give her enough credit."

After a long silence, he nodded. "You're right."

Ethan could see Joan's motivation not telling Doc, but it was a hard call. "Do you think you would've quit school like she feared?"

"I don't know. I think I would've tried to continue in school with the scholarship I got. Maybe we could've made it. But I'll never know, will I? Joan didn't give me that choice."

Doc stood. "Good night." He walked into his room and shut the door.

Ethan let himself out. He scanned the parking area looking for Tessa, but didn't see her. He walked to his truck and put his hand on the door handle, but paused. Leaving while not knowing if Tessa was physically okay didn't sit well with him.

He walked around the barn and scanned the open corrals behind the stables. Tessa sat on a bale of hay, her arms wrapped around her knees. She wasn't crying, but she looked lost.

She must've heard him, because her head came up.

"Go away, Ethan."

"I will, I promise. I just wanted to make sure you were okay with all the trouble we've been having."

Standing, she nodded. "Thanks."

"If you need to talk, call me."

"I don't know what I need. Good night, Ethan."

He wanted to push her, to fix her problems, but knew in his spirit this was not the time. He nodded to her and walked back to his truck, praying for her.

As he drove home, he knew her heart would need time to take in what she'd learned. He was still reeling from the revelations tonight, too.

A lot of naked truths had come to light and no one knew how to deal with them.

"Father, we all need Your grace and wisdom, because I don't see any good way out of this mess. You can take the ashes of our lives and make it into something good."

He'd have to cling to that truth in the coming storm.

He would need it.

Chapter Twelve

Tessa sat on the bale of hay, watching the sky. She heard Ethan's truck pull away from the clinic. Her world had come crashing down around her head tonight, shattering the truth she'd held on to. Her feelings remained numb. Encased in ice.

If she thought about what she'd learned, she might go running into the night, screaming at the top of her lungs.

Each time her mind latched on to one of those new truths, her heart shut down. If she remained numb, then she wouldn't have to deal with the lies and cover-ups.

She buried her head in her knees. Oddly enough, Ethan's presence at the table had been a steady pillar that had propped her up. She'd held his hand, a touchstone in the midst of the storm.

"Oh, Father God. I'm lost. What is happening here? I don't understand.

"Why?"

Resting her chin on her knees, she felt the wave of pain and confusion wash over her.

Her mind foggy, she heard a horse's whinny. She released her knees and got off the bale of hay. She followed the sounds of the horse's restlessness.

Lady stood in her stall. The horse seemed to be dreaming. Hope stood beside her mother. Tessa slipped into the stall and ran her hands over the mare's side. "Hey, girl. You reliving bad times?"

The horse woke and looked back at her.

"You and your baby are safe now, Lady." Tessa moved around to the horse's head and rubbed her nose. Lady was almost unrecognizable with all the weight she'd gained. Hope woke and wandered up to her mother and began to nurse.

Horses, Tessa understood. She would've said

before tonight that she understand people, too. But now, she couldn't claim that.

Tessa leaned against the stall wall and slowly slid down. Her eyes fluttered closed and sleep quickly swallowed her.

When Joan walked into the kitchen the next morning, she looked around for Tessa. Vince stood at the stove, making pancakes.

"Have you seen Tessa?" Joan asked, panic rising in her chest. "She never came to bed last night."

"She's in the barn. Asleep."

Joan glanced in the direction of the walkway. She wrapped her arms around her waist. "I stayed up to talk to her, but she never came in. I got worried about her, wondering…" She looked at Vince. "I don't know what to say."

Vince poured a cup of coffee and handed it to Joan. "Give her time. It's a big shock to her."

Joan turned to him, her eyes filled with tears. "I did what I thought was right, Vince. I couldn't take your dream away from you, and I knew you wouldn't leave me if you knew. I wanted you to have that dream."

Doc tossed the last pancake in the frying pan onto a plate and brought it to the table. He also snagged the plate of sausages from the warming shelf on the stove, carrying it to the table. Butter and syrup were there, too. "You didn't give me that chance, Joan. You turned my dream into a hollow reality. I would've found a way."

"You think so now, but you don't know if you could've made it. And if you'd failed, would you have ended up hating me for getting in the way? Would we have ended up hating each other?"

He rested his hands on the chair back. "We'll never know." A muscle in his jaw jumped as he stared across the table at her. "Instead, I spent the last thirty years alone, longing for the woman I loved above all else."

Joan gasped and put her hand over her mouth. Tears made tracks down her face. She shook her head as if to deny the hurt she'd caused and ran back into her room. The door slammed behind her.

Doc collapsed into one of the kitchen chairs. He ran his hand through his white, thinning hair. He didn't want to hurt Joan, but he couldn't tell her she'd done the right thing. She'd made her decision unilaterally and the more he thought about it, the madder it made him.

And he'd been robbed of knowing his daughter, who was an astonishing vet. He'd spent most of his life alone. After being raised in a one-bathroom house that he shared with eight other people, he'd ended up living alone, with two bathrooms and a stable full of animals. In terms of wealth and position, he was much better of now...and yet his life was so lonely.

It didn't seem fair. He looked down at the two plates of pancakes and sausages on the table. He didn't have an appetite. He put two plates back on the warming shelf just in case anyone wanted something to eat.

Looking at the clock, he saw that it was time to get ready for church. Maybe he'd find some answers there.

But first, he wanted to check on Tessa.

Tessa finished her rounds in the clinic part of the barn. They had three horses, a goat and a momma cat who'd wandered into the clinic, ready to deliver her babies. So far, momma cat's time hadn't come.

As she looked in the stall, she saw the cat lying there, her five kittens by her side. Tessa squatted and studied the babies.

"So your time came, did it, Momma?"

The cat raised her head.

"They all look in good shape. Mind if I look?"

The cat relaxed, as if sensing Tessa meant no harm. Tessa gently picked up one of the kittens. A tiny meow issued from the tiger-striped ball of fluff. "Okay, let me just check you out," she told the kitten.

After a quick examination, Tessa gently laid the kitten back by his mother's side. Tessa quickly checked out the rest of the babies. Just as she put the last kitten by her mother, Tessa felt someone behind her.

"How are they?" Doc asked.

She didn't look up. "They look healthy. But I think we need to put some food out for the mother cat. She hasn't complained, but she's going to need some nourishment."

"I'll get it," Doc whispered.

As Tessa waited for Doc to return, she knew she wasn't ready to talk to him. She wasn't ready to talk to anyone. That didn't make sense, but her head and heart were still reeling.

"Here it is."

Tessa stood and moved out of the stall. Doc placed two dishes on the floor.

"I added some liquid vitamins to the food."

A good idea. They didn't know where the cat was from. They'd scanned her and she didn't have a digital chip.

"Tessa, I don't know what to say," Doc began.

She looked at the man who she had discovered was her biological father. "Doc, I'm not ready to talk about anything right now. And I don't think you are, either, so why don't we postpone this discussion for a while?"

He didn't readily agree. "I understand, Tessa, but we are going to have to face it, and probably the sooner, the better."

She gritted her teeth.

"I know your mother isn't ready to face the issue."

She nodded.

"I made breakfast. It's in the kitchen."

The thought of food turned her stomach.

"It's Sunday. I think maybe a trip to church might help the situation."

Making eye contact with him, she wanted to make sure she heard him right. "Church?"

"Yes, church. You might not be able to talk to me or your mother, but there's Someone who would understand and help."

"I don't know."

"Be ready in twenty minutes. I'll drive." He didn't wait for her to respond, but turned and left.

I'm not ready, she wanted to yell at Doc's retreating back. Resting her head against one of the support beams in the stable, she closed her eyes. She wasn't going to go anywhere, yet she found herself walking into the house. The smell of coffee came as a welcome distraction. She poured herself a cup, grabbed a sausage, wrapped it in a pancake and walked to her room to get dressed.

When Ethan wandered out into the kitchen that morning, he saw his parents reading the Sunday paper.

"So how'd it go last night?" Ken asked his son.

Ethan didn't answer. Instead, he walked to the coffeemaker and poured himself a cup. His mother had left the baked egg casserole in the oven to keep it warm. He didn't want to eat, but grabbed a biscuit and left the kitchen.

He walked down the hall into the den and looked out through the big, plate-glass window at the mountains in the distance. He hadn't slept but a few minutes. Instead, he'd ended up praying through the night for Tessa.

Their date, which had had such wonderful promise, had blown up in a way he never could've imagined. He still couldn't believe that Doctor Adams, Vince, was Tessa's father. He could barely digest it. Doc had a daughter and hadn't known it. Ethan understood how hard it was for Tessa to understand it. He could barely take it in.

"Is something wrong, son?" Ken walked up beside Ethan and paused.

"I'm sorry I didn't answer you earlier. I was distracted." He turned and tried to give his father a reassuring smile. It came out pathetically.

Ken took in a deep breath. "Does this have something to do with your date last night?"

Ethan felt as though he couldn't tell his father Tessa's and Doc's secret. It wasn't his secret or his story to tell, but he needed to say something to his father. "I learned some things last night, Dad, but I don't feel like I can talk about it." He took a sip of his coffee.

After carefully studying his son, Ken nodded. "I won't ask you to betray someone else's confidence."

"But that doesn't mean you can't pray, Dad, for the situation."

Ken patted Ethan's shoulder. "That's what I admire about you, son. You can keep someone's secret, yet you don't walk away from the responsibility."

His father's praise made Ethan feel about two inches tall. Ethan didn't feel he deserved the praise because he'd not been honest with his parents. "Thanks."

"You coming to church?"

"After asking you to pray, I think I better

show up, too." Besides, he wanted an excuse to see Tessa and see how she fared.

Tessa sat in the main sanctuary. They'd missed the Sunday school classes, but made it in time for the second service. She hadn't wanted to come, but the tension between her mother, Doc and herself nearly suffocated her. Here, at least, there were other people.

Ethan slid into the pew beside her and grabbed her hand. "How are you?" he whispered.

"I don't know," she answered back.

He glanced around Tessa and acknowledged her mother and Doc.

The keyboard player began the opening praise chorus.

Tessa remembered nothing of the service and automatically greeted the people around her. Ethan's family surrounded them. They teased Ethan about his talent roping a calf, then asked how the date went.

"Fine," Tessa automatically answered.

"Please come out to the ranch for dinner again," Lynda offered. "We'd love to be able to have you and your mom join us."

Tessa's phone rang. Opening her shoulder bag, she answered it. "Doc, it's Randy Cousins. We've got a horse down here. One of the rescued horses."

"Okay. I'll be there ASAP." Closing her phone, she told the group what had happened.

"I'll go," Doc volunteered.

"Not this time. If you'll drop me by the clinic, I'll take my truck out there."

Doc opened his mouth, but Tessa shook her head. "If I'm going to take over here, I need to do this."

The older man remained quiet for several seconds, then nodded. "You're right. I'll take you out to the clinic."

"Let me," Ethan spoke up. "That way, I can talk to Randy myself and we can notify the sheriff of another problem with the rescued horses. I can also notify Mary, too."

Doc nodded. "Okay."

Ethan took Tessa's arm and guided her out to his truck. He'd decided before church to drive because he wanted private time with Tessa.

On the trip to the clinic, the inside of the truck remained quiet. Tessa welcomed Ethan's big comforting presence beside her, not demanding answers or asking how she felt.

When the clinic appeared, Tessa relaxed. He pulled in next to her truck.

"Let me get some extra supplies from the hospital."

He leaned out of his driver-side window. "Are you sure you can reach all the supplies you need?"

His question snapped her out of her dark thoughts and she remembered that first moment of awareness between them. She smiled at him. "Yes, Mr. McClure, I can reach all the things I need."

"I was just making sure. Do you want me to take the lead in going to the Cousinses' ranch?"

With all that was on her mind that was the smart thing to do. "Yes." She hurried inside. They needed to get out to the Cousinses' ranch. She didn't know how long the horse had been down and every second counted.

Colic had the horse rolling. Tessa, Randy and Ethan got her up and started walking her.

"Last night I found this hay on the ground

out in the corral out back where Sugar—that's what we've named her—was kept. What caught my attention was the hay was thrown in the dirt just outside the fence. When I saw that, saw her eating it off the ground, I grabbed her and put her in the barn. Coming back to the hay, it didn't smell right.

"I thought I caught Sugar before she ate too much of it, but when I came back to check on her, Sugar was sweating and nipping at her belly."

Studying the horse, Tessa asked, "So she ate that hay last night?"

"Yeah."

"You still have some of it?"

"Yeah, I have it in that trash can on the side of the stables."

"Good. I'll take some of it and analyze it." Tessa ran her hands down the side of the mare, then pulled out her stethoscope from her bag and listened to the horse's middle.

"Okay, Sugar, let's see if I can give you some medicine and help you with that mess in your gut."

Tessa gave the horse a shot and then took her

halter and started walking her around the corral. Over the next couple of hours, they took turns walking the horse until Sugar seemed to be doing a little better.

Randy told Tessa he'd call if they needed her again.

"I'll stay."

Randy shrugged his shoulders and walked inside.

As Tessa walked the horse, she called out to Ethan. "You don't have to wait. I can find my way back home."

Ethan fell in step beside her. "I know you can probably find your way. I just want to stay."

Tessa turned her head and looked at him. "I'm okay, Ethan."

She wasn't, and he knew that. "Do you object if I stay?"

"Why?"

Sugar snorted and shook her head.

"Easy, girl," Tessa crooned to the horse. Tessa ran her hand along the horse's flank. "There's some churning there."

She resumed her walking of the horse. "So tell me, Ethan, why do you want to stay?"

"What you learned last night was enough to throw anyone off their stride."

She looked away, silently making it clear she didn't want to talk.

"I thought you just might need the support of a friend."

Her expression said she doubted that was really his reason, but she didn't insist on him leaving. Ethan knew Tessa needed him, even if she wouldn't admit it.

Randy and his wife, Sharon, appeared out in the yard. Each of them carried a bowl. Sharon called out, "I've got some stew for you two. I know you missed lunch, Dr. Grant."

"Tessa, please call me Tessa."

"Why don't you eat, Dr. Tessa, and let Randy walk the horse."

Tessa opened her mouth to refuse, but Ethan answered for them. "Sharon, thank you for thinking of us." He took the bowl from her hand.

Randy traded Tessa the bowl of stew for the horse's lead. Both Ethan and Tessa sat on the bench outside the stables. Sharon walked back into the house while her husband took over walking the horse.

Ethan and Tessa ate in silence. Sharon appeared again with two coffee cups and set them on the bench beside them. Ethan nodded his thanks.

"Have you called the clinic, updating Doc on what is going on?" Ethan asked once they were alone.

"When have I had time?" she answered tightly.

He didn't comment, just pulled out his phone and called the clinic.

Tessa understood she was using this case of colic to avoid talking to her mother and Doc. She'd have to deal with the truths she learned last night, but she didn't want to try today. *Lord, help,* she prayed.

She took over walking the horse from Randy. "I want to keep her moving to see if that mess in her intestines will break up," she explained to Randy.

"Okay."

"And be sure to get me that hay. The sheriff might be interested in it, too, so you might want to gather another sample for him."

Randy got a paper sack and put some of the bad hay in it. He brought it to Ethan.

"I thought Sugar was out of the woods." Randy shook his head as he watched from outside the corral. "I should've kept better watch on her."

"Did any of your other horses eat that hay?" Tessa heard Ethan question.

"Oddly, no. It was as if someone planted that hay just for Sugar." The instant the words were out of his mouth, Randy turned to Ethan. "That's what's been happening with all the fostered horses, isn't it?"

"It's only happened one other time, but the hay was planted for the fostered horse to eat it then, too."

"We need to do something about William and his buddy beyond the restraining order." Randy folded his arms over his chest.

"I'll call Mary and see if we can get another rescue group to finish fostering these horses."

"I was thinking the same thing," Tessa called out.

Randy leaned close to Ethan, but his words carried in the still afternoon. "I think Doc Adams sure picked a good associate. First time I saw her, I wasn't so sure. I guess that old saying is true, you can't judge a book by its cover."

Tessa's heart warmed. They continued taking turns walking Sugar over the next few hours. She needed to pass the bad feed. Close to five in the afternoon, Tessa suggested they might try loading the mare into a trailer.

Ethan and Randy gave her funny looks.

"You sure, Tessa?" Randy asked.

"It's an old trick I learned from the foreman at the place where I housed my horse."

Randy shrugged, but brought around his trailer.

"Now load her into the trailer."

Randy's brow shot up but he got the horse up into the trailer.

"Okay, now unload her," Tessa called out.

Ethan cocked his head. "What are you doing?"

"I'm helping Sugar."

Randy backed the horse out of the trailer.

Suddenly, her system started working and nature took its course. The horse bobbed her head and seemed to smile.

Both men started laughing.

"Dr. Tessa, you're a genius." Randy kept eyeing the horse. Sugar's head was up.

Tessa sprinted to her truck and pulled out a large container of a common dry laxative. "Dust that on her hay. It should help any other issues. And I'd say to leave her out to pasture, but if you're going to move the horses, just be sure to give her plenty of water."

Tessa gathered up her things. Ethan helped.

"Would you like to stop and get a burger at the Dairy Mart?" he asked.

She considered his offer. It was the perfect excuse not to go home and face the problems there. "Okay." As he turned away, she added, "Thank you, Ethan."

"I'm here for you, Tessa. Don't doubt it."

Heaven knew, she needed someone.

Chapter Thirteen

Ethan called Doc once he was in his truck and updated him on what had happened with the horse and where they were going.

"I'll need to contact Mary, see about moving the horses. And I'll talk to William."

"Are you sure that's a good idea, Ethan?"

"I think I know what's driving William, and if I'm right then he needs help." All the signs were there, yet Ethan had ignored them.

"How's Tessa doing?"

"She refuses to face anything. She's not ready."

"I'm sorry to hear that." Sadness colored the words.

"How are you and Joan getting along?"

Ethan worried about how Doc was handling the situation. Ever since Ethan had known Doc Adams, the man had been a steady, dependable presence. He had a dry sense of humor and didn't tolerate shading the truth. But he'd kept Ethan's secret.

"We're avoiding each other. I'm nervous trying to talk to Joan because my normal compass seems to be facing the wrong direction. I don't know what to do."

"Are you sorry you hired Tessa, Doc, and brought her into your life?"

There was a long pause. "That's a good way to think about it, Ethan. Thanks."

"I know it's not easy, Doc, but would you rather not know the truth? Would you have wanted to never know about your daughter?"

"I would've liked to have known I had a daughter from the start."

"But that didn't happen."

Doc didn't reply.

"I'm sorry, Doc. This has to be hard for you."

"You're right, Ethan. I can't change the past, but I can build a future with Tessa."

"Amen to that," Ethan answered.

They quickly said goodbye and hung up. Ethan sent up a prayer that maybe he could have a future with Tessa, too.

Doc hung up the phone.

"Who was that, Vince?" Joan asked, walking out of the bedroom where she'd closeted herself.

He turned toward the only woman he'd ever loved. "Ethan. They've finished at the Cousinses' place. Ethan said that they are stopping for a burger. I think he's going to try to talk to Tessa."

Joan stumbled toward the kitchen table. "I thought my past was buried." She sighed. "Now, suddenly it's exploded in my face."

Vince sat across from Joan. "It's amazing how sometimes our past catches us."

Joan stared at the plastic checkered tablecloth on the table. Vince could see how Tessa resembled her mother. And he could also see his own mother's traits in his daughter.

His daughter.

His heart swelled with pride. "She's an amazing woman."

Joan's head came up and she locked eyes with his. "She is. Never did she complain about how things were as she grew up. Even when we lost the ranch, she didn't whine." Joan's eyes took on a faraway look. "It made my life so much easier. Tessa never blamed me for Warren's behavior—until last night." Her gaze came back to his. "Do you blame me?"

"Joan, I can't say. I'm still reeling from learning the truth."

She didn't challenge or accuse him. "There was never a day that I didn't wish things had turned out differently. When Warren disappeared and we lost the ranch, I thought the world had come to an end.

"Tessa and I scrambled, but you know, it was one of the best things that ever happened to us. I got a job, went back to school. Tessa worked to keep her horse and decided what her future would be." She smiled at him. "She inherited your love of animals and your way with them. I was so proud of her."

"She's got talent and I believe she's going to be a great vet. It's her size that throws everyone."

Leaning forward, Joan rested her elbows on the table. "You know, I admired the vet who hired Tessa. That man saw past her height to her potential. Now, knowing who hired her, I'm not surprised.

"For years after Tessa was born, I wondered what my life would've been if I'd married you. Even after I married Warren. Finally, after we'd had a particularly bad fight, I made a conscious decision to stop thinking about what you and I could have had. It wasn't fair to Warren or Tessa and it made me sad. I think he knew I never successfully got over you and that's why he started drinking. I apparently ruined a lot of lives."

"We do what we must."

"Yeah, but it was no comfort." She traced an imaginary line on the table. "Did my dad really run you off with a shot-gun?"

"He did. After that, I just finally gave up."

"He wasn't an understanding man. He missed knowing his granddaughter."

Vince winced. "Did you ever reconcile?"

"I tried once. He wouldn't bend and wouldn't forgive me. I knew I couldn't expose Tessa to him. My grandmother made up for Dad's shortcomings. She was great for Tessa. Until she died when Tessa was ten, she'd have Tessa come and spend a week with her during the summer. She spoiled her outrageously. When I asked her about how her daughter could've cut her grandchild out of her life, Grandma just shook her head and said she thought she'd raised a stronger child than that."

Not knowing anything about her family but the few things Joan had told him that summer long ago, Vince gobbled up every piece of information she gave him.

"How's your family?" Joan asked. "As I recall you had lots of siblings."

"I'm the only one who left the mountains. They've all managed to come out here to visit, but I'm the black sheep of the family. No one really understood why I left except for my mother. She encouraged me to follow my dream."

"I wanted that, too, for you, Vince."

He understood her reasoning. It was a valid reason. Too bad his heart didn't agree.

* * *

Once Tessa and Ethan arrived at the drive-in and ordered burgers, they sat at one of the picnic tables outside and ate.

"You were good with Sugar today," Ethan told her. "Wonderful and patient."

She put down her burger, her face somber. "I understand horses and how to take care of them, but I don't understand why—" She pushed the burger away. When she raised her head, her eyes glistened with tears. "Suddenly, everything in my life is a lie. My father wasn't really my father and the story my mom spun about my life wasn't the truth. And the place where I've come to establish my career is the house of my biological father.

"It's like my entire life has been cut off its moorings. I don't know if anything my mother has ever said to me is true."

Ethan grabbed her hand, pulled her to her feet and wrapped his arms around her. "Tessa, you're in the middle of a storm. Don't try to understand now. Just give yourself time, and let the Lord comfort you."

She tipped her head back. "How?"

The back of his fingers stroked her cheek. "Every time you start thinking about the situation, sing your favorite chorus or hymn. Send up a prayer."

"That easy?"

"Probably not, but it's a plan. Keeping busy might be useful, too—maybe you can help me try to get organized to move the rescue horses. I'll call Mary tonight and see if we can arrange it."

"Call her now."

Seeing Tessa concentrate on something beside her parents gave him a boost. "Okay. I'll make the call."

It took less than ten minutes for Mary to like the idea. She told him to stand by while she made some calls. When Ethan hung up, Tessa smiled at him, the first smile he'd seen since that fateful moment when they'd walked into the kitchen.

"So, she's going to arrange it?" Tessa asked.

"She is."

"There's light at the end of the tunnel."

"There is."

Ethan finished his burger. Tessa still fiddled

with hers. "Wait here." He threw the words over his shoulder as he opened the door to the drive-in and ordered two ice cream cones. When he returned, he held out one cone to Tessa. "I thought you might like this."

Her eyes watered. "You remembered."

Laughing, he nodded. "I couldn't help but notice. You're a girl who likes her ice cream."

She took the cone and started licking it.

Before they finished, Mary called back. "It's set. Tonight you and I will call the ranches fostering the horses and tell them the plan."

"Thanks, Mary. You just email me which of the ranchers you want me to contact." When he hung up, he smiled at Tessa. "It's all set."

"Then let's see how fast we can get these horses away from here. I want to make sure all the horses and ranchers are safe."

He walked her to her truck. "I'll drive behind you to make sure you get home okay."

"You don't have to do that."

He cupped her cheek. "I know you are capable, but still you're not as familiar with this area as I am and it's getting dark. I'd feel better if you let me do this."

She studied him, thinking. "Okay."

As they drove off, Ethan wished he could protect her emotionally as well as physically. He couldn't, but he knew Someone who could.

The closer she got to the clinic, the more Tessa's muscles tightened. She didn't want to face her mother and Doc. She wasn't ready.

Looking into the rearview mirror, she saw the lights of Ethan's truck. The man had been a steady presence over the last nightmarish day. Was it really less than twenty-four hours since she'd walked into the kitchen and heard her parents arguing?

Her parents.

Her mother and her father.

How strange to think of Doc as her father. She'd come to know him as a colleague and admired his skill as a vet. Oddly, they thought the same way about horses and how to approach them. He'd evaluated her talent, not her gender or size.

And he was her father. It was more than she could take in.

She pulled into the clinic parking lot. Ethan

parked beside her. Before she could get out of her truck, he was at her side, opening the door. "You want me to go in with you?"

Before she could answer, the back door opened and Doc appeared in the walkway. "How'd things go?"

"Tessa kept after that horse until the colic passed." Ethan threw her a grin. Pride shone in his eyes.

Doc nodded. "You think that's going to happen again?"

"We can't take that chance. We're going to move the horses to the rescue group out of Taos."

Tessa cocked her head. "So they called you back?"

Ethan nodded. "They did while we were driving back. Mary's making final arrangements. The group in Taos will find good homes for the horses with all the rich folks and celebrities that run through that place."

Tessa gathered up her equipment. Doc joined her, taking several bags from the bed of her truck.

"Ethan, do you want to stay for a cup of coffee?" Doc asked.

"I can't, Doc. I've got a lot of work ahead of me to arrange to move those horses."

Doc nodded and left Tessa alone with Ethan.

"If you need anything, call me," Ethan whispered to her before he brushed her lips with a kiss.

Tessa watched as he drove away, knowing that she'd need to gather her courage and face her parents.

When she went inside, no one was in the kitchen or living room. She went to her bedroom and found her mother packing her suitcase.

Her mother looked up from the bed, but said nothing before she resumed her packing.

Carefully, Tessa put her purse on the dresser. She needed to say something, but didn't know where to begin. Her mind was still mired with a thousand conflicting feelings with not a clear thought in sight. "Why are you leaving?" she asked at last.

"I got a call from my company. There's been a hitch in the deal I negotiated last week and I need to fly back to Brussels. My flight home leaves at 5:30 a.m. Vince has agreed to drive me to the airport in Albuquerque. I'll catch a flight the next morning at 7:30 for Brussels."

Tessa's legs gave out and she sat on the bed. "I could—" Her cell phone rang and she retrieved it from her purse. "Yes, Ethan?"

"I've got several volunteers together to help drive the horses to Taos. Since the clinic is centrally located, we're going to meet there at seven in the morning. Will you be able to oversee the horses, and talk to the others in the group?"

Looking at her mother, she said, "I don't know. There's been an emergency and Mom needs to fly out early tomorrow morning. I don't know if I'll be back in time."

Joan waved to her. "Vince is going to take me. If you need to do something, don't let my leaving stop you."

It was a logical solution to the dilemma, but it wasn't the right one. She nodded to her mom. "Ethan, Doc is going to cover the airport run, so I'll be here."

"Call me if you need anything, Tessa."

"Thanks," she whispered and hung up. When she looked up, her mother said, "Tessa, we need to talk."

Joan walked to the other twin bed and sat facing her daughter. "I know you're still upset. It's been only twenty-four hours since you learned the truth." She glanced down at her hands. "I've pretty well messed things up, but you need to remember, I thought I was doing the right thing. My father felt I shamed the family. I was supposed to 'get rid of the problem'. I couldn't do that, and my father didn't want me back if I kept you. But you were the only thing of Vince I had left and I couldn't give you up.

"I loved Vince so much." Joan grasped Tessa's hands. Looking down, she worried her bottom lip. "I should've just had you and lived with my grandmother, but I really did think that Warren and I could come to love each other and you could have a normal family. My marriage wouldn't be that head-over-heels love I felt for Vince, but a soft kind of love between close friends.

"Warren thought he could live with that. I

was honest with him, Tessa. I never lied to him. But it turned out that Warren couldn't live with the truth. In the end, he wanted more from me. And no matter how hard I tried, that love never blossomed. I knew why he started gambling and drinking and I felt responsible for driving him to that. I don't think he would've done what he did if he'd never met me.

"And I couldn't tell you. How were you going to understand that Momma didn't love Daddy?"

The emotional churning inside Tessa wanted to erupt, but she knew if she said the things in her heart, she would forever drive her mother away. So instead of responding, Tessa sat silently.

Her mother released Tessa's hands and sat back. Her eyes darkened with pain. "I made bad decisions, Tessa, but at the time, they seemed the best choices." She fell silent.

"Mom—" She opened her mouth, but nothing else came out. She wanted to say something, reach out to her mother, but the wound was still so raw, aching. Tessa stood and walked into the bathroom as tears slid down her cheeks. The last thing Tessa heard was, "I'm so sorry."

Closing the bathroom door, Tessa tossed her smelly clothes on the floor and turned on the shower. Stepping into the streaming jets of water, she grabbed the shampoo, poured it into her hand and scrubbed her head. As she rinsed the shampoo from her hair, water as well as tears streamed down her face.

When she finished her shower and slipped into her pajamas, she turned the light out in the bathroom and walked out into a dark bedroom. Joan lay in the twin bed, her eyes closed. Tessa knew her mother wasn't asleep, but she didn't say anything.

Climbing into bed, Tessa turned to the wall. She tried to empty her mind of all thoughts, but the first line of Psalm 31 kept running through her mind. *In You, O LORD, I have taken refuge; let me never be put to shame....*

Ethan hung up the phone after talking to Randy Cousins, the last rancher he needed to notify of the move.

He pinched the bridge of his nose. It had not been the best of days. His phone rang. He snatched it up, thinking it might be Tessa.

"Ethan," Mary began.

His heart deflated.

"I just finished my last call," she continued. "I'll bring the final instructions with me when we meet at the courthouse in Los Rios tomorrow."

"Sounds good. Thanks for the update." He wasn't in the mood to chat, particularly with Mary.

He started to hang up when she said, "Ethan."

"Yes?"

"Uh, I—well, we've never really talked since—"

He'd spent so long dreading this conversation, but now that it had come, he realized that his reluctance was far outweighed by his need to get through with it quickly so the line would be free if Tessa needed to call him. "No, we haven't, but you don't need to explain, Mary. You've done a lot with your life since that day. You should be proud of yourself."

"I should've said something to you. I tried, but I always chickened out."

The hurt that still lived in his soul evaporated. Like a puff of smoke, it was gone. "You did. I just wasn't listening, Mary. I knew something was wrong that Thanksgiving when I came home from college. I should have listened to my heart and Heaven."

He heard her sigh. "I want you to know something, Ethan. You are a good man and I think you and Tessa are made for each other. It won't make me feel bad to see you two together. Really, it would make me happy to see you happy."

He nearly fell out of his chair, her declaration leaving him wordless.

"You don't have to say anything, Ethan. I just wanted you to know. See you tomorrow." She hung up without giving him any time to respond.

He looked at the handset in his palm. What irony. He had an ex-fiancée giving him permission to court Tessa, who was so hurt and mad she didn't know what she was doing or feeling. "Lord, what is going on?" The world seemed upside down.

Tessa heard the engine of a truck rumble to life. She looked at the digital clock on the nightstand. 3:30 a.m. Her eyes fluttered closed, then she remembered her mother was leaving with Doc. She threw off the covers and ran through the kitchen and out into the breeze-way. She saw the truck pulling out of the park-ing area.

She rested her head on one of the crossbars bracing the mesh screen. "Oh, Mom." She walked back inside, feeling numb, and sat in one of the chairs.

What was she to do?

She felt like she was staring into a void.

Her gaze moved around in the kitchen. Make coffee. She could do that. After she started it, she moved into the barn and began checking on the horses there.

Her first stop was Lady's and Hope's stall. "Hello, Momma, how are you doing today?"

Lady's tail twitched. Hope woke and came toward Tessa. "Hello, young lady," Tessa addressed the filly. Tessa slipped into the stall and stroked Hope's head. Looking at the baby, Tessa realized how hard it was going to be to give the filly and her mother away. Tessa felt alienated from her mother, and the first foal she delivered as a practicing vet would be leaving. She buried her face in Hope's side, fighting a wave of overwhelming despair.

Vince glanced at Joan, who sat on the other side of the cab of his truck. Her misery washed over him as he sat behind the steering wheel.

"She'll come around," he said.

Joan slowly turned her head toward Vince. "Will she?"

"Just give her time, Joan. It's been a shock to her."

"What about you, Vince? Do you hate me, too?"

He tried to concentrate on the road before him, but it became fuzzy through the moisture in his eyes. "No, Joan. I don't hate you. But I keep wanting to go back and do it all again. Why didn't I put two and two together back then?"

"So you didn't have any idea?" she pressed.

"I feel like a dope, but no, I had no idea. I guess I was just an insecure kid from the hills. Of course, your dad hinted that you'd run off with someone else." He shrugged. "I was too gullible to see he blamed me for the situation."

Joan put her hand on Vince's arm. "He didn't want to live with the shame of his daughter getting pregnant out of wedlock. I thought he was so strict because he was just old-fashioned. But he only cared about how it made him look. My mother took his side.

"That night before I went to my grandmother's, I wrote you a letter, telling you everything, pouring out my heart to you. But I didn't mail it. You were going to make something of yourself, have a wonderful career, marry and have a good life. I loved you so much that I wanted all of that for you."

If she only knew. He'd become a vet, but without ever having a family and wife and kids. He led a satisfying life, but not a rich one. Not the one he'd wanted. He couldn't tell her that her sacrifice had only made everyone's life miserable.

"Vince?" She reached out for him again.

"I'm trying to understand, Joan. You acted out of love."

"But?"

"We can't go back and change the past, but we can start from here and go forward."

Joan didn't appear convinced.

"I had a horse I was treating right after I came here. I thought the horse was suffering from colic and that with a little time and medicine he would be fine. Turns out I completely missed the diagnosis. When the owner went out the next day, the horse was dead. I felt responsible for that horse's death. For a while, I thought about giving up until Ken McClure came to me and told me he understood that I'd made a judgment error, but it didn't have to be a career ender. Ken believed in me. He wanted me to change the future, because there was nothing I could do about the past. I've never lost another horse to colic.

"Joan, all we can do is pick up the broken pieces of our lives, learn from them and go on." Vince turned onto the road to the airport. "Tessa is who she is because of what she went through. I'd like to think her natural talent with animals comes from me, but who knows? Maybe it was from her spending time working to keep her horse fed, or seeing how the people at the stables cared for the animals. I don't know. What I do know is I'd like to keep her as a partner and be part of her life from now on." He threw her a glance. "And maybe explore a relationship with Tessa's mother."

Joan remained quiet for a long time as she studied his profile. Finally, she said, "I'd like that."

He nodded. "I just hope Tessa can move forward, too."

Chapter Fourteen

Tessa stood in the barn and watched Lady and Hope. She'd let her heart become attached to these two. She knew she needed to move them, but something inside her rebelled at the notion.

The phone in the barn rang. Getting a call this early in the morning wasn't unusual. Tessa answered it.

"Hey, Tessa," Ethan said, "I just got a call from the other rescue group. One of their members had something come up and can't participate, so they can only take seventeen of the horses. We need to leave three of the horses here. I figured you might want to keep Lady and Hope. Will that work for you?"

A gift from Heaven. She choked back her tears. "Yes, that'll work."

His wonderful laugh came through the line, comforting her. "I thought that might be the case. Of course, Lady and Hope are the horses Kevin and William want the most."

"True, but we can face them. No one else need put up with the harassment."

"I'm also going to alert the sheriff, let him know what's going on. I'm keeping the horse I had, but we're still going to need you to drive to the Cousinses' ranch to pick up their rescue horse."

"I can do that, but I want to wait for Doc to come back to be with the horses before I leave."

"Don't worry about that. I've notified the other ranchers we're changing the time and meet-up place. We'll meet up in Los Rios and leave there around ten-thirty."

"I'll be there."

She hung up and heard footsteps behind her. Turning, ready to fight, she found Doc standing inside the door.

"Your mom's on her way."

Nodding her head, Tessa turned to go.

"Tessa, wait."

She stopped and turned to Doc.

Slowly, he walked to her. "When your mother showed up here several days ago, my world blew apart. So many things fell into place. Why she suddenly disappeared, why I recognize something so familiar in you and why things clicked between us. I felt comfortable with you—your mannerisms and how you did things were so familiar. I marveled at it.

"I've tried a couple of times to get young vets to come out here and join the practice. The last time I tried was maybe five years ago. He lasted probably a month. He and I continually got in each other's way. He thought I was old-fashioned and just plain weird. It was a relief when he decided he needed to practice in a major city somewhere else. We both were fine with his decision."

She wanted to laugh, but clamped it down.

He read her stifled reaction and grinned back at her. "But this last time I got kicked, I was at the McClure place, and we all knew I needed a young partner. The difference this time is I did some praying." He rubbed the back of his head. "I called some of my old friends at Purdue and asked about a candidate to come out here. Dan Melcher suggested you, said you were a special vet who had talent. He did note your height. It didn't matter because if you worked out, it wouldn't be an issue.

"What I wanted—and what I got—was a good associate. The last thing I expected was to find a daughter, and one of whom I'm very proud."

His words were welcomed, but she knew things weren't going to be resolved today. "I don't know what to say."

"I'd like for you to stay and continue working here."

Tessa hadn't even thought about leaving, but how would staying work out? "I think I'd like that."

His shoulders sagged and he nodded. "Let's just take one day at a time."

"Okay." Tessa explained to Doc about the change in plans for the rescue group and that Lady and Hope were staying. "I'm glad we can keep them. I think I've lost my heart to those two and would like to keep them here."

"That's fine, but be careful. You can't keep every distressed animal you treat," he warned.

He was right. Her professors at Purdue warned them not to take in every stray, abused animal. Their job as vets was to treat the animal, not keep it. "I know, but horses are my weakness, and I used up my one time right out of the gate." Besides, she needed to focus on something or someone else other than the unexpected news that turned her world inside out.

"I understand."

She didn't doubt he did. "Thanks."

Five of the volunteers in the rescue group met in the parking lot of the courthouse in Los Rios. A couple of the trailers held three to four horses.

Mary had driven from her office in Albuquerque to the rendezvous place. "We'll meet the other rescue group outside Taos. There's a veterinary clinic on Highway 86 south of the city. Taos Veterinary Clinic is the name. Any questions?"

No one spoke up.

"If that's the case, let's go." Mary looked at the horses in the trailers. "I don't see the mare and her filly."

"That's because the other group called early this morning and said they couldn't take all our horses. I asked Tessa if she wanted to keep those two. She did," Ethan explained.

Mary looked from Ethan to Tessa. Mary wasn't obvious in her expression, but Ethan read Mary's satisfaction. "You know the risks with William and Kevin?"

"I do," Tessa quickly answered. "But I feel that Lady still needs some medical care. And I want to adopt them."

Mary folded her arms across her chest. "I hope you won't regret it, because as I recall, those are the ones Kevin wanted."

"I understand."

Ethan moved to Tessa's side. "If need be, I can stable the horses for a short time, leaving the clinic safe."

Raising her hand, Mary shook her head in

surrender. "Okay. I'll get the paperwork going for you, Tessa, to adopt the horses. Just be careful." She turned to Ethan. "I've got court this afternoon, so when you're nearing Taos, give Sheila Green a call and let her know how far out you are. She should have all her people there to transfer custody of the horses. Let me get the papers from my car."

"I'm serious, Tessa," Ethan warned, once Mary left. "If you have any more trouble from Kevin or William about Hope, let me know. We can stable the horses at our ranch."

"Are you changing your mind from this morning?" Tessa replied.

Laughing, he said, "No. I would've adopted them if you hadn't."

"You're serious?"

"I am."

Mary joined them with the papers and handed them to Ethan. "Good luck."

As they departed from the city, Ethan felt a glimmer of hope that Tessa would survive the blows she'd received over the past several days. Her love for Hope and Lady was strong, steady, showing him she was a fighter. Given time, she'd find her footing. He prayed that was the case.

The next few days Tessa worked herself into exhaustion, falling into bed each night dog-tired. She took as many of the calls as she could, driving out to the ranches to check on cattle, horses and a variety of cats, dogs, rabbits and a couple of snakes. Each time she stopped to think about the truth surrounding her birth or her emotions tried to erupt, she followed Ethan's advice and sang a worship chorus.

Knowing her feelings were out of control, Tessa avoided discussing the situation with Doc. He was having his own problems, dealing with the truth. How should they treat each other? Their relationship couldn't remain as it had been before.

Tessa was in her office when Mary called the clinic.

"Hey, Tessa. Could you come to my office in Albuquerque? I've got the adoption papers for you to get custody of Lady and Hope. It can wait until you can get away, but you'll need to sign those papers."

It was a good excuse to leave for a while. "Sure, I'll come today. When do I need to be there?"

"Two o'clock would be great. I have a brief hearing at two at a smaller sub-courthouse, but that should only take five minutes. We could meet in the lobby."

"Where is it?"

Mary gave her directions to the building the city was using until they could add on to the main courthouse.

"I'll see you."

At two, Tessa appeared in the lobby.

Mary hurried in. "Great, you're on time. My hearing's up the stairs. It won't be long, then afterward, we can walk to my office and you can sign the papers to get Lady and Hope," Mary explained.

"Okay."

As they walked up the stairs, Mary asked, "Is everything okay?"

Tessa stopped and stared at Mary, panicked

that maybe Ethan had talked about her situation with his ex-fiancée. "Why do you ask?"

"You seem a little unsettled and I noticed some tension between Ethan and you last week. I just wanted to reassure you that I don't have a problem with you seeing him. You and Ethan seem to be a good match. I'm happy for him."

"Oh." Tessa felt odd having Ethan's ex encourage her. Was her attitude so bad that Mary noticed? "I'm just having a little trouble adjusting to everything. You think things are going well and then suddenly it seems like you've run into a wall."

Mary nodded. "I understand perfectly. The morning of my wedding, I ran into that wall."

True to her word, Mary was done in five minutes. Tessa accompanied Mary back to her office across the street from the sub-courthouse and signed the papers, taking custody of Lady and Hope.

As Tessa walked back to her car, she saw Ethan and William Moore go into the side entrance to the church on the corner across from Mary's office. What was going on? She'd been blindsided one too many times, and she needed to know what was happening.

She walked across the street and went to the side entrance. The church proper was built high, with steps leading up to the first floor. There were five steps down to the side door. Tessa walked down the steps and went inside. She heard voices coming from an open set of double doors. She followed the voices.

Looking inside, she saw people wandering around the room. Several were huddled by the table with an industrial-size chromo coffeepot, including Ethan and William.

"Hello," a woman cheerfully greeted Tessa. "Welcome to our meeting. Won't you come in?"

"What kind of meeting is this?" Tessa asked.

"This is the Gamblers Anonymous meeting."

Shock held Tessa motionless. Looking over her shoulder, her eyes met Ethan's. The blood drained from her head.

Tessa slowly became aware of the woman talking to her. She came out of her stupor and faced the woman. "Thanks. I'm in the wrong place." Somehow her legs carried her outside. Ethan didn't follow her.

How she made it back to the clinic, what roads she drove, she had no idea. She just remembered parking her truck outside the clinic and walking to the corral to look at Lady and Hope. The instant Hope saw Tessa, she trotted over.

"Hello, girl," Tessa greeted, reaching out to the filly.

Hope stretched her neck, enjoying the attention.

Tessa closed her eyes, as the pain of seeing Ethan at that meeting with William Moore washed over her. Ethan was at a Gamblers Anonymous meeting, which meant he was a gambler.

"Lord, what is happening?" she whispered, her heart completely shattered. "Everything in my life has disappeared. Why, Father? What is going on?

"You are my only constant. Please help." She rested her head on the top rail of the fence, despair swamping her.

As Ethan drove toward the clinic, his heart pounded as if he'd spent the last hour running.

When he'd run into William Moore a couple of weeks ago, William had been coming out of a bar, a gaunt, haunted look in his eyes. Ethan recognized the expression—a gambler who'd lost money.

God had moved in Ethan's heart and he'd reached out to William. Over a sandwich and a cup of coffee, William had told a familiar story about being sucked into gambling and getting in over his head. He owed Kevin Raney a lot of money and had promised Kevin Lady's foal in recompense. To make things worse, his mother had sold the foal to someone else right after William made his promise. But when the rescue group seized the horses, he panicked. His ace in the hole was gone.

Ethan had offered to take William to the Gamblers Anonymous meeting that was held at the church across from the sub-courthouse in Albuquerque. This was their second meeting. The moment Tessa stumbled into that church basement room, Ethan knew any future he had with her had vanished. She wouldn't "bet" on someone who had a problem with gambling.

He wanted to at least explain to her what she'd seen.

Pulling into the clinic parking lot, Ethan noted that only Tessa's truck was there. He walked into the house, calling her name. Silence greeted him.

He checked the clinic/office, then the stables. Still he didn't find her. His heart raced. As he turned to search the house again, he saw the open barn door. He slipped outside and saw Tessa leaning against the top rail.

The relief made his knees weak.

She must've heard him, because she turned to face him. The look in her eyes stopped Ethan in his tracks.

"Tessa, I need to explain some things to you."

He'd seen *that* hurt in her eyes when her mother had told her the truth. It killed him to see it directed his way, but he prayed she'd stick around long enough to learn the truth.

She didn't argue or yell but folded her arms around her waist and waited. She seemed cold and remote as if watching him from a distance.

Her reaction frightened him. Was she beyond any explanation? "I'm William Moore's sponsor in the GA group. He's found himself trapped by his gambling, and I reached out to him. That was his second meeting."

A muscle in her jaw flexed. He didn't think she'd say anything, but she finally asked, "Don't you have to have been a gambler in order to sponsor one?"

"Yes."

He could've sworn the temperature had dropped into a subzero range. A killing silence hung between them.

"Why don't you sit down." He pointed to the bale of hay. "My story's not short."

Her gaze went to the bale, then where he stood. He backed up a couple of steps. "I promise I won't come closer."

She eyed him, then the bales. After a moment of consideration, she walked to the bale and sat.

Give me the words, Lord, because I don't think I can do this with just my strength. "Like I told you, I rodeoed in high school. I thought I was a big hotshot. My junior year, I was doing pretty good. The summer between my junior and senior year, my parents allowed me to travel the rodeo circuit with a sponsor. Kevin Raney was there and sidled up to me, flattering me and telling me I was the next star. He said I needed to meet the in-group, power players on the circuit, and he introduced me to the 'elites.' After a couple of times of hanging with them, they invited me to join their 'friendly' game of cards. I won that first night. I was doing so well Kevin told me I could really increase my money by getting into the betting pool, which bet on the different rodeo events.

"Before I knew it, I was five thousand dollars in debt to him."

Tessa's eyes narrowed and he read the condemnation in her expression.

"At the end of the summer, Kevin demanded his money. He threatened to go to my parents for it." The painful memories flashed through his brain. "I didn't realize how far in debt I'd gotten, but I didn't want to disappoint my parents. Besides, the ranch was going through a rough time with the drought and my dad having to sell off stock." Shame washed over him again. "I was here at the clinic, when Doc noticed the cloud over my head. He asked me about it, and I spilled my guts."

Ethan sat on the bale of hay beside Tessa, but didn't look at her. Instead, he rested his arms on his thighs and laced his hands together, staring at the ground. "Do you know what Doc did? He made a deal with me. He'd pay Kevin, but I had to work off the debt. He made me promise never to gamble again if he helped me." He took the chance and turned his face toward Tessa.

Her expression told him she was listening, but he had to tell her more.

"It took me close to a year to pay off my debt, but true to his word, Doc never said anything to my parents." He sat up. "The entire time I worked here, Doc made me pull my weight and talked to me about never repeating my mistake."

"So why were you in that meeting with William?" Tessa asked.

"Because I knew William had a gambling problem. When we were in high school together, I knew he ran wild and drank and gambled. I saw William a couple of weeks ago after he took a bad beating from some of Kevin's friends. I couldn't walk away and not try to offer a helping hand to him.

"He grabbed it. He went with me to the meeting. So now I'm William's sponsor—that's the only reason why I was there."

"I wish I could believe that, Ethan. But I had a father—no, no, a stepfather—who claimed he wasn't gambling. Several times, he said he was on the straight and narrow, until the bill collectors showed up at our house." The memories caused her to shake. "At one point we were sure he finally got it all together, was attending the GA meetings, until the day he said he was going to a GA meeting and simply disappeared. A week later the sheriff and the new owners showed up at the house."

He opened his arms, needing to hold her. She leaned back, out of reach, and shook her head.

His heart ached. "I understand your doubt, but I never gambled again. Ask Doc."

Her expression didn't change.

"I couldn't walk away from William without

extending the mercy to him that Doc showed to me."

Slowly, she stood. "Ethan, I've been down this road before and I don't have the faith to believe." She walked into the stables.

Her words were like a punch to his gut that nearly doubled him over. He stared out into the paddock at Hope prancing around and investigating her world. The filly's joy for life should've made him smile, but his shattered heart wouldn't allow it.

She was cold. And it had nothing to do with the outside temperature. She felt frozen inside. Every emotion, every thought, every prayer, every breath. Her heart was so far into the deep freeze, she wondered if she'd ever get warm again. But if she thawed, and let the turmoil inside her break loose—well, she didn't know if she'd survive it. This way, at least, she could function.

Or pretend she could function, because at this moment, she didn't believe she could.

Chapter Fifteen

Ethan walked around the outside of the barn toward his truck. He wouldn't go through it, because he didn't think Tessa wanted to see him again.

He'd expected yelling and accusations from her but her cold, lifeless reaction worried him even more. If she yelled, he could deal with the anger, but the cold was deadly.

As he rounded the final corner of the barn, Doc pulled his truck into the parking lot. Doc slowly climbed out of the front seat. "What's wrong, Ethan? Was there an accident? Is everyone okay?"

"Tessa saw me walking into the Gamblers Anonymous meeting this afternoon with William. When I came by to see her and explain, she confronted me with it. I told her about what happened with my gambling. She listened, Doc, but I don't think she believed me." Misery swamped him. "She told me about her stepfather relapsing and she doesn't trust me to not gamble anymore."

"Ethan, look at me." The sharp command cut through Ethan's fog.

His gaze met Doc's. "With her world blowing up around her, I think you were a solid presence for Tessa. Now she's been shocked again with the one issue that is most critical for her. Give her some time and space to get her bearings. She's a smart woman and, given time, she'll find her balance."

They were words of hope, but Ethan had his doubts. "I pray you're right, Doc. She's been burned badly, and I don't know if she's willing to open her heart again, especially to a man who's had a bad brush with gambling."

"I understand, but remember God can move mountains and change the heart of a young woman."

Ethan would have to hold on to that thought, because his prospects didn't look good.

Joan's call came at six in the morning two weeks later.

"How are you doing, Tessa?" Joan asked.

Tessa sat at the kitchen table, Doc across the table from her. They'd come to an uneasy truce and were able to work together, but they didn't speak about the uncomfortable truths that had come to light. "We've been busy around the clinic."

The line hummed with silence.

"I should be here in Amsterdam until the end of the week."

"Okay."

"You're still upset with me," Joan stated.

Tessa didn't want to discuss the subject, especially with Doc so close. "I'm still numb and don't know what to think. Or feel. I'm trying, but—"

"I understand, but Tessa, the longer you refuse to deal with the emotions in your heart, the harder it's going to be. I know. If I'd confronted Warren the first time he came home drunk, our lives would've been different. Or if I'd told Vince I was pregnant and trusted him and our love, who knows what our lives would have been.

"I have lots of regrets, sweetheart. Please, don't make my mistake. Will you consider that? Pray about it?"

Tessa felt the first crack in the ice encasing her heart. They'd been through so much together, how could she ignore her mother's plea? "Okay, Mom, I'll try."

When Tessa hung up, she looked up into Doc's face. He held out a refilled cup of coffee to her. She took it.

"Your mom?" He nodded toward the phone.

"Yes."

He poured himself another cup of coffee and sat down at the table. "How is she?"

"She's fine."

After taking a sip of his coffee, he asked, "I'm still in awe of finding her after all these years." He wrapped his hands around the mug. "These last few days, I found myself wondering what our lives would've been if Joan had told me about you."

The ice cracked more. "I think I would've liked that."

They remained silent, lost in their individual thoughts. After a minute, Doc rose. "I'll help you clean up." The person who cooked didn't clean, and he'd cooked this morning, but she was willing to accept the gesture.

"Sure."

They worked together.

"During the summers," Doc stated, "Ethan would come to the clinic and help me on Fridays. At one time, he thought he might like to be a vet."

She paused in putting dishes in the dishwasher. "So what happened that changed his mind?"

Doc put the butter in the refrigerator. "You really want to know?"

Did she? "Yes."

He leaned back against the counter. "Those years ago, when Ethan was looking for a college to go to, he had his problem with gambling. It rattled him so much, that something inside him shifted. I think he discovered he had feet of clay like the rest of us. He knew if anyone discovered what he'd done, they'd be disappointed. But the person he disappointed the most was himself.

"He couldn't tell his parents, and Mary wouldn't understand. Also, with the shortage of cash his parents faced, he knew there was no way he could pay the expenses to become a vet." He fell silent. "It took a long time for him to come to peace with what he'd done, then Mary stood him up at the altar."

Tessa's heart ached for Ethan. The man may have had a wonderful family, but he'd taken his share of lumps.

"Ethan hasn't repeated his mistake, Tessa. And he's extended mercy to others who faced the same problem he did." Doc started another pot of coffee. "William isn't the first person that Ethan's taken to a GA meeting. I think he's helped several others to stop gambling." Doc leaned forward. "Tessa, the man has not ever gambled again. He learned his lesson and I know he doesn't want to disappoint his family again. I think you can trust him. I do."

Tessa sat down at the table and considered Doc's words. "Thanks for telling me."

They rang in her mind and heart for the next few days. She found herself wanting to talk to Ethan about how Lady and Hope were doing. Or ask him if he'd heard from the other rescue group on how the horses were faring.

Ethan didn't call or come by the clinic, leaving Tessa listening for his truck and wanting to see him. She couldn't come up with a good excuse to go out to the McClure Ranch. But the ice around her heart was melting, leaving her to feel.

One afternoon, Sophie called the clinic and asked Tessa if she could come to their place and look at the horse she'd doctored earlier.

Tessa readily agreed.

When she arrived in the early afternoon, Sophie was in the stables, the baby asleep in the ranch office. When Tessa asked where the horse was, Sophie picked up the sleeping baby and put the child over her shoulder.

"I don't want you to wake the babe. If you'll just direct me to where Dakota is, I'll fill you in after I see him."

"Not to worry, this little darling can sleep

through the worst thunderstorm and not wake. Besides, I thought you and I could talk."

Warning bells went off in Tessa's head, but she didn't argue. Tessa wanted to pick Sophie's brain anyway.

They walked through the stables and out the side door to the corral. The gelding stood in the corral, eyeing them when they walked out. He moved away from the fence. Suddenly, in midstride, Dakota started limping.

Tessa frowned and opened the corral gate and walked to the horse. He danced away.

"He's a tease," Sophie offered.

Tessa stopped, set down her bag and opened it. She rummaged around at the bottom and pulled out one of the peppermints she carried. She stood and slowly pulled the cellophane off the candy, holding it up where the horse could see it. Dakota stopped his pacing and whished his tail.

Both women waited as the horse decided if he wanted the candy. He approached, but there was no limp in his gait. Tessa allowed the horse to lip the candy and she grabbed his halter.

The horse happily ate the candy while Tessa pulled a strap out of her bag and clipped it to the halter, then tied the horse to one of the fence posts of the gate.

"Okay, boy, let's see if you have anything wrong with your hoof." Tessa ran her hand down the back leg, feeling the muscle. She could detect no abnormalities. Grabbing his hoof, she pulled it up and looked at the frog. It looked healthy. She repeated the exam of all the other hooves. Everything looked normal.

Standing, she ran her hand down his back. "I think you're a big faker." Tessa glanced at Sophie. "You have a smart boy who likes to pull one over on you. The next time he comes up with a limp, give him a treat. I think you'll find he's okay."

Tessa untied the horse, unclipped the strap and patted him on the rump. He wasn't interested in leaving, wanting instead to look for more candy in her bag. Tessa pushed the horse's inquiring face away from her bag and closed it.

"Sorry for the false alarm," Sophie said.

"But I'm glad that big tease got you over here. I wanted to talk to you."

Tessa's stomach jumped, but she pasted a smile on her face and let herself out of the corral. "What did you want to talk about?"

"Ethan."

Every muscle in her body tensed. "Okay."

"Why don't we go up to the house? That way we won't be disturbed."

Tessa followed Sophie into the main house. After Sophie laid the baby down in the playpen in the kitchen, she fixed two iced teas and brought a bag of chocolate cookies.

Sophie took a bite of the cookie and closed her eyes. "I'm afraid cookies are going to be my favorite thing this pregnancy."

Tessa's look of surprise quickly turned into a broad smile. "I didn't know. Congratulations."

Sophie put her finger to her mouth. "Shh, I haven't told anyone yet."

"Not even Zach?"

"Particularly not Zach. He'll act like I'm breakable, and I've things I need to do and don't want to argue with him."

"I understand." Tessa couldn't stop smiling.

"But that's not the reason I wanted to talk to you. What happened between Ethan and you?"

The humor left Tessa's face. "Why do you ask?"

"Because I've never seen the man so miserable and the only thing that's changed is he isn't spending time at the clinic. I know it's not because of Dr. Adams."

Tessa didn't know how to answer.

"I know it's not my business, but with all these hormones running around in me, I want everyone to be happy." She reached out and put her hand on Tessa's forearm. "It's the mother in me."

"We didn't have an argument," Tessa started to explain.

When she didn't continue her explanation, Sophie jumped in. "Ethan was very instrumental in helping my husband deal with losing his leg when he was in Iraq. The man was a pillar of strength and didn't give up when Zach pushed everyone away. Ethan is the one person that everyone turns to when things get rough.

"I've seen lots of single women smile at him, and let him know that they're interested, but he hasn't responded. That is, until you showed up."

"I didn't give Ethan any flirty looks."

Sophie grabbed another cookie. "I know. You messed with his horse, instead."

That caused Tessa's eyes to widen, then she grinned. "He was rather testy."

"I know. If you're anywhere close by, Ethan's gaze is on you. I watched him at the dinners you've come to at the McClures' ranch and at church and his gaze never leaves you. Lots of people who know Ethan have commented to me that it looks like the last McClure male is going to fall."

Tessa didn't know where to look.

"I've rejoiced for my brother-in-law and friend. Then suddenly, Ethan's face looks like the world is coming to an end. He's in pain, Tessa. Whatever it is, I think you should talk it over with Ethan and give him another chance. He's a wonderful man."

Tessa didn't want to discuss any of this, but in her spirit, she knew this was her opportunity to talk to someone. Doc's view of Ethan was colored by his feelings for the man. "How long have you known Ethan?"

"Maybe three years or so."

"Have you ever seen him gamble?" Tessa asked.

Sophie's eyes widened and her jaw dropped. "No. I've never seen him do anything like that."

Maybe Sophie didn't know her brother-in-law as well as she thought. "At school, during football or basketball seasons, you know how people bet on the games. Did he do that with his brother?"

Sophie opened her mouth to answer but paused. "No. He hasn't ever joined any betting pools like that. Is that the problem that came up between Ethan and you?"

Could Tessa risk it? "My fa—my family lost our home when my stepfather's gambling debts came due. I don't ever want a repeat of that in my life."

"Oh, Tessa, that's terrible, and I can see why you'd be wary of any man who gambled, but Ethan doesn't have that problem."

She wanted to believe Sophie, but sometimes

gamblers were very clever at hiding their addiction. "Then why did I see Ethan going into a Gamblers Anonymous meeting with William Moore?"

"Are you sure?"

"Yes. I asked him about it. He admitted that he wanted to help William by taking him to a meeting."

"But that doesn't mean he's a gambler himself," Sophie argued.

Tessa didn't reply.

They heard the doors of a car slam, then Zach and Ethan walked into the house.

"Hey, honey," Zach called out, walking through the living room. When he saw Tessa, he stopped. "Tessa."

Ethan stopped behind him.

An uncomfortable silence descended.

"I called Tessa to look at the faker, who acted like he had another rock in his hoof. He didn't."

"That horse is smart and lazy. I gave him a peppermint and he suddenly could walk. There was nothing in his hoof." Tessa stood. "If he comes up acting like he is lame, just give him a candy. If that doesn't work, call." Grabbing her medical bag, she walked out of the house, passing a tall, silent Ethan. She fought to keep from looking at him, because if she did, she might break down in hysterical tears.

"Tessa," Ethan called out. He followed her outside. Walking into the house and seeing her nearly knocked him off his feet. He wanted to talk to her, hear her voice.

She paused, allowing him to catch up to her.

When he did, his eyes ate up her face. How much he'd missed her. "How are you doing?"

"I'm making it."

"Are you talking to Doc?"

"Yes, we're talking." She reached her truck door and opened it, putting her bag in the backseat on the floor. She climbed into the driver's seat and closed the door.

He'd picked up the phone half a dozen times and started to call her, but had hung up. He'd also prayed for her, that her heart could open up and she'd forgive her parents and him.

"Give Doc a chance. You'll be glad you did."

He saw moisture gather in her eyes. She nodded and opened her mouth as if to say something. Her lips snapped shut. She started her truck and drove off.

He didn't know how long he stood there, but suddenly he felt Zach's hand on his back.

"What's going on, bro?"

Ethan turned to his brother. He knew his family would worry until they knew the real reason Tessa had withdrawn from him. Now was the time to reveal the deep secrets of his past.

"Let's go inside. I've got an ugly story to tell you."

They walked inside and sat down at the table across from Sophie.

"You remember the summer between your freshman and sophomore years? You did so well on the rodeo circuit that midway through the summer, our uncle came and convinced Dad to let him take you to some rodeos in Montana and Nevada where the prize money was better. He said it would help you with college, since the ranch had started having money troubles."

Zach rested his elbows on his knees. "Yeah, I remember."

"I stayed and did some small rodoes in state and in Colorado." Ethan swallowed. Words stuck in his throat. "I came in second place in the calf roping. I got my money and suddenly Kevin Raney showed up."

Zach sat up straight.

"I was feeling like a loser, coming in second. I wanted the first-place prize money to save for college and to maybe help Dad. Kevin appeared at my side, saying he thought I did a good job, then asked if I wanted to double that money. I did that night with poker. And the night after that. But my winning streak didn't last long."

With each word, Zach's expression turned grimmer. Sophie's eyes filled with understanding and sympathy.

"By the end of the summer, I was in debt to Kevin for five thousand dollars." Ethan couldn't look at his brother anymore, so he stared down at his hands. He explained the deal he'd made with Doc, finishing with, "I never gambled again."

Waiting for his brother's reaction was the hardest thing that Ethan had done in a long time.

Zach stood up and pulled his brother to his feet and hugged him.

"I'm glad to know I wasn't the only son who had feet of clay," Zach whispered. When he pulled back, he patted his brother on the cheek. "Your explanation makes a lot of things you've done make sense."

Ethan could only marvel at his brother's reaction. It lifted a lot of guilt off his shoulders.

Sophie stood and reached out to Ethan. "I'm glad you told us. I hope Tessa will understand that we all make mistakes. None of us are perfect."

"She told you? About her family?" Ethan wanted to make sure that Sophie understood about Tessa's stepfather.

"She did."

If she told Sophie, then maybe there was hope. He prayed there was.

Later that night, Ethan sat down with his parents and told them his secret. Neither parent seemed surprised. His dad nodded his head.

Ethan looked from his mother to his father. "Is that your only reaction?"

"What do you want us to say?" his mother asked.

"You're not shocked or disappointed?"

"Son," his mother said, "we knew something had happened but didn't know what. I wanted to talk to you, but your father wouldn't let me. We prayed for you, that God would shine His grace in the situation. He did. Doc brought you up short."

Ken rubbed his chin. "Why are you telling us now?"

"I knew if William Moore was hanging around Kevin, he had a gambling problem. I saw him one day in town, and talked to him. I ended up taking him to his first couple of Gamblers Anonymous meetings. Tessa saw me and followed me into the meeting. She is very anti-gambling and confronted me. I explained why I was helping William but ever since then she hasn't been sure she wants to continue seeing me."

Ken and Lynda traded looks.

"Did you explain that you've not gambled again?" his dad asked.

"I did."

"And?" his mother asked.

"She doubted me."

Lynda stood and kissed Ethan's cheek. "Then she doesn't know you. If you want to talk, get a woman's perspective, I'll listen." She left the room.

His dad continued to sit at the table.

"I can't believe you knew and didn't say anything," Ethan muttered.

"It wasn't easy for your mom, but I kept her from pushing you about it. We just didn't know exactly what your secret was. When you announced that you would work for Doc that summer I talked with him, asked if there was anything I needed to know. Doc assured me things were fine. I don't doubt if you hadn't turned around, Doc would've come to your mother and me." His eyes locked with Ethan's. "What I think is you now have to let go of the guilt, son. It's time to forgive yourself."

The words struck a deep chord in Ethan. "I—"

"We all foul up and get it wrong. Stop beating yourself up. Remember, God has forgiven and forgotten those sins. So should you. And I think maybe Tessa shares that trait with you. She needs to forgive." His father stood and walked around the table, rested his hand on Ethan's shoulder and squeezed.

As Ethan watched his father walk out of the kitchen, a sense of relief washed through him. He hadn't realized how much keeping that secret had crippled him. But was it true that he hadn't forgiven himself for his mistake?

"Okay, Lord, I'm going to give You this guilt. And I forgive myself." He remained still, his soul finding a wellspring of peace.

His head dropped forward. "Thank You, Lord."

Having the load lifted from his shoulders, he prayed that Tessa could find her footing among the new truths she'd learned.

Tessa wrestled with her feelings all through the night. Seeing Ethan yesterday had been both joyous and painful. She'd wanted to reach out to him, talk to him about Doc, the rescue horses they transferred and half a dozen other things. Suddenly, there was someone in her life she could freely talk to. And yet, he'd gambled.

When she woke the next morning, her lack of sleep showed on her face. Doc took one look at her and volunteered to drive them to church. She didn't argue.

During the song service, Tessa kept looking across the sanctuary to where Ethan was sitting with his family.

When the congregation sat for the message, Tessa felt a longing in her heart. As she prayed, she heard the pastor talking about the Prodigal Son.

"Who suffered more in the end?" the pastor asked. "The son who came back and repented or the son who stayed and was mad his father forgave his brother?"

The words pierced the last remaining layer of ice around her heart and feelings flooded her chest. Was she that older son, the son who remained, who couldn't forgive? She glanced over at Ethan. He turned his head and met her gaze. She was the first one to look away.

Then Doc's phone vibrated with an incoming text. He showed it to Tessa—he was needed at an emergency. They slipped out of the sanctuary and went to Doc's truck.

On their drive back to the clinic, Doc glanced over at Tessa. "I'm surprised that you and Ethan didn't burn up several of the pews in the sanctuary."

Tessa, still thinking about the sermon, turned to Doc. "What?"

He smiled and glanced at Tessa. "Remember, I was between you and Ethan. More looking I've not seen in a long time. I thought I'd have to duck not to get scorched by the flames."

Rubbing her arms, she looked down at her lap.

"Tessa, I don't want to see you repeat the same mistake that your mother and I made."

Her eyes widened. "I'm not pregnant."

"No, I didn't think you were, but I think you might be blaming Ethan for the sins your step-father committed."

She opened her mouth to argue, but knew Doc was right.

"Although I've not been around for most of your life, I wanted to talk to you as a friend.

I think you can trust Ethan not to repeat his mistake."

She wanted to believe that. Could she? Was it that simple? "Thanks, I'll think about it."

Tessa waved goodbye to Doc, grabbed her Bible and her notes from the service and walked into the stables. Odd, how much clearer she could think in the midst of the horses she loved. She looked up the scriptures Pastor had used and reread the story of the Prodigal Son.

Was she blaming Ethan for the sins of her stepfather? After several moments of facing the truth, she knew that that's exactly what she'd done.

The truth of her actions made her ashamed. Was she judging her mother in the wrong light, too? And what about Doc? Wasn't he completely innocent in the situation?

Her behaviour over the past week came back to her, shaming her. "Okay, Lord. I've been wrong. Forgive me." As she prayed, she thought of all the people she'd hurt over the past few days. She had a lot of folks she had to talk to so she could make amends. And even if she couldn't contact him directly, she had to include her stepfather in that forgiveness.

As she walked into the kitchen, the clinic phone rang. There was an emergency at the Cousinses' place. They needed her to come right away. As she hung up the phone, Tessa knew she'd have to make a lot of things right.

Oddly enough, she looked forward to it.

Chapter Sixteen

"I wonder why Doc and Tessa left early," Beth commented as the family sat down at the dinner table.

Zach shook his head. "I don't doubt that there was an emergency."

"So why did Tessa leave with Doc?" Beth asked.

"Maybe they came in one vehicle," Tyler, Beth's husband, answered.

"Go and see the woman," Zach encouraged Ethan. All conversation stopped.

"I'm not sure she wants to talk to me."

Zach choked on his tea, nearly spitting it out. Setting the glass down, he stared at his brother. "Are you kidding me? I saw those looks you two were exchanging during the message. I thought you might make up and kiss in the lobby of the church. I think Pastor might have been tempted to halt his sermon, call you two to the front and start a wedding ceremony."

Ethan glanced around the table. Every head nodded in agreement.

Ethan's gaze scanned each face. He saw encouragement from everyone. Before their meal, Ethan had told Beth and Tyler of his gambling problem. His family stood squarely behind him.

He stood. "You've convinced me."

"You gonna call first?" Beth called out.

"Nope. Why give her a chance to say no?"

Beth stood and raced around the table and gave him a kiss on the cheek. "Good luck."

"Thanks, sis." He turned to leave.

"And if she gives you any static, call me. I'll straighten her out."

Ethan just shook his head. If he let Beth get to Tessa, there would be no hope. "Thanks, but I think this is something I need to do myself."

* * *

When Tessa returned to the clinic after the call she made, she saw her father's truck parked in the clinic's parking lot.

Her father.

The shock of that thought robbed her of breath. Doctor Vince Adams was her father. The thought still astounded her.

She pulled in next to Doc's truck, turned off the engine, and stared out the front windshield.

Deep in her spirit, she knew calling Doc "Dad" was the right thing.

Dad.

Before she could open the truck door, Kevin Raney pulled his truck and horse trailer behind hers and Doc's trucks.

Tessa scrambled out of the vehicle. "What do you think you're doing?" she demanded.

Kevin shot out of the cab. "Shut up." The man looked as if he'd run into a wall, with a black eye and split lip. He had a crowbar in his right hand.

"Who do you think you are?" Tessa stopped and glared at him.

"I'm the man who's going to take his horses."

Kevin reached for Tessa's arm. She tried to dodge him, but she turned her ankle on a piece of gravel. Kevin caught her and jerked her close. "I'm through fooling around with all you do-gooders, messing with my horses. All you've been is a pain for me and my associates. That filly is mine and, for my time and the hassle you put me through, I'm taking the mare, too."

Tessa didn't doubt his bruised and battered face had something to do with his attitude.

Doc appeared at the kitchen door. "Whoa, what's going on here?"

"Back off, Doc. I'm here to take my horses."

Doc nodded toward the crowbar. "Horses don't respond well to that."

"True, but people do. Now let's all go into the stables and get the horses."

Tessa's eyes went to Doc's face. He appeared calm, not cowed by Kevin. "You in trouble?" Doc asked.

"I'm not here for socializing or for you to try to figure me out. I came for my horses."

His hands up in surrender, Doc answered, "Fine, let's go and get the horses, but I don't think you need to drag Tessa into the stables that way."

"She's my insurance."

Doc's gaze met Tessa's. Kevin pushed Tessa toward the stable's door. As they neared where Doc stood, Kevin became more agitated. When Doc lunged for the crowbar, Kevin drew his arm back and hit Doc in the head. He went down hard.

"Dad," Tessa cried out, trying to lunge out of Kevin's hold.

She didn't break his hold, but was jerked back.

"Dad?" Kevin's brow shot up. "Dr. Adams is your father?"

Tessa's chin came up and she glared at him, but didn't respond.

"That puts a whole new spin on things, don't it?" He looked from Doc to Tessa and his eyes narrowed. "If you don't want to see me hit him again, let's go and get my horses. When I drive out of here, then you can tend to the old man."

Tessa's gaze left her father and met Kevin's. His battered face and determined look left no doubt in Tessa's mind that Kevin was desperate enough to follow through on his threats.

"Okay."

Kevin hauled her into the stables, leaving Doc bleeding and unconscious on the ground.

As Ethan drove to the clinic, he prayed that Tessa's heart would be ready to embrace a new future with him. He might not win her trust, but he had to try. He shook his head at the irony.

What he wanted was a chance with the remarkable woman he'd come to know. And every family member supported his decision. Apparently they recognized the truth—that he and Tessa belonged together.

As he turned down the short drive to the clinic, he saw two people out in the parking lot. One person was trying to load Lady into a horse trailer.

Ethan stopped at the end of the driveway, blocking the way of escape, and got out of his truck. Kevin and Tessa stood at the back of the trailer. Tessa held Lady's lead reins. Ethan didn't say anything, but observed Doc lying very still on the ground, his arms splayed and his forehead bleeding.

"Well, lookie here. It's our hero riding to the rescue." Kevin had a crowbar and kept beating it into his hand. The moment anyone moved, Ethan didn't doubt that Kevin would bash in Doc's head.

"What's going on here?" Ethan knew exactly what was happening, but he needed to divert Kevin until he could come up with a plan.

A satisfied grin crossed Kevin's face. "Please, Ethan. It's obvious what's going on here. I'm getting my horses—" Ethan opened his mouth to answer, but Kevin continued on "—and no one's going to stop me."

From Kevin's battered appearance, it was obvious that the man's creditors weren't happy. Ethan's first priority was to keep Tessa safe. Raising his hand, he said, "Hey, no problem."

His answer didn't win over Kevin. "I don't believe you. You've always got to be the hero, don't you? Things were going great and suddenly Mr. Hero appears and saves William." A bitter laugh escaped his mouth.

Tessa's gaze flew to Ethan's. He saw the

surprise turn to gratitude in her expression. "Look, Kevin, the quicker you're out of here, the better for you. You know as well as I do that things don't stay quiet around here for long. And I have the sneaking suspicion that my family's going to show up soon."

The words worried Kevin as he looked toward the dirt road. "Why don't you get back in your truck and park it beside Dr. Grant's car, then give me the keys."

Ethan's main goal was to get Kevin away from Doc and Tessa. "All right." He walked back to his truck and backed up. As he did, he grabbed his cell phone and called for help. The operator replied and as quietly as he could, he relayed the situation. "And don't call back or he'll know." Before the woman could ask any more questions, he cut off the phone call and shoved the cell under the front seat.

Ethan left the truck and handed his keys to Kevin. "I'll help Tessa load the horses so you can get away from here faster."

"I don't think so." Kevin thought for a minute, then changed his mind. "Let's do it this way. I'll have the lovely doctor stand over here with me while you finish loading the trailer with both the mare and her filly."

Ethan didn't like the idea of Tessa in range of Kevin's anger, but Kevin didn't let him close enough to yank the crowbar away. Slowly Ethan walked to Tessa and took the lead reins from her. He gave her a reassuring smile. Tessa whispered, "Thank God you're here."

"Cooperate," he whispered back.

She gave him the reins and their hands briefly lingered.

"C'mon, Dr. Grant, unless you want me to hit Doc Adams again with the crowbar."

"I'm coming."

Ethan made sure Tessa was okay before he finished walking Lady into the horse trailer. After he secured the horse in the trailer, he walked back out.

"Now, go get my filly."

Given no choice, Ethan complied and quickly got Hope out of her stall and put her into the trailer. "Now, you've got both horses, why don't you drive out of here."

Scratching his chin with his left hand, Kevin

appeared to think about it. "I don't know. Taking Dr. Grant would insure that you'd behave."

"Taking Dr. Grant would mean that law enforcement could charge you with kidnapping, not just the misdemeanor of stealing the horses. And with your record, the misdemeanor would be easier for law-enforcement officials to swallow."

Anger filled Kevin's face and Ethan tensed, ready to lunge to disarm Kevin before he could harm anyone. "Stand over there by Doc Adams."

Ethan moved to stand above Doc. Kevin dragged Tessa with him to the driver's side of the truck. "Open the door," he instructed her.

She did. He pushed her away and jumped into the cab of the truck, turned on the engine and pulled around in the parking lot. Tessa hurried to Ethan's side. His arms wrapped around her and Ethan felt some of the tension in his gut ease.

As Kevin finished his U-turn and started out of the parking lot, a sheriff's vehicle pulled into the drive, blocking Kevin's way of escape.

The sheriff immediately got out and pulled his gun.

"Stop," Joe Teague yelled.

For an instant, it looked as if Kevin wasn't going to stop. Finally, after a moment of hesitation, he did.

"I want to see your hands, Kevin," Joe commanded.

Kevin put his hands up. Ethan went to the truck and opened the driver's door.

"Get out, Kevin, and walk toward me," Joe ordered.

Ethan stood ready to wrestle the man to the ground if he tried anything funny. Kevin complied.

"Put your hands on the hood on my car," Joe instructed.

While Joe cuffed Kevin, Ethan turned toward Tessa. She knelt at her father's side.

"Dad," Tessa said as she checked the older man. Looking up, she said, "Help me roll him over."

Together they gently rolled Doc onto his back. A large gash skirted the older man's hairline. She jumped up and ran to her truck, grabbed her medical bag and was back, kneeling at his side.

Doc moaned and brought his right arm up to his eyes.

"Take it easy, Dad," Tessa murmured. She grabbed a sterile gauze pad and lightly blotted his forehead. Doc grimaced.

"I'm sorry," Tessa whispered.

Doc's eyes fluttered open and he turned toward her. "I'm okay, but I've got a humdinger of a headache."

Sitting back on her heels, Tessa gave her father a watery smile. "I'm so sorry."

"Why?" Doc whispered.

Closing her eyes, Tessa's chin tipped up. "I don't know. For being so childish and pouting. You didn't have any control over what happened in my life before I came here."

He reached up and cupped her chin. "It was the greatest blessing of my life when I found you. And that was before I knew you were my daughter." He started to grin, but grimaced. "I'm glad that horse kicked me in the leg."

"Amazing how God can work in any situation." She grasped her father's hand. Looking

at Ethan, she said, "Let's get him inside, unload the horses, then I think we've got a trip
to the emergency room in our future."

Tessa sat in the E.R. waiting room, Lynda
McClure at her side.

Lynda shook her head. "I can't believe you're
Doc's daughter."

"I can't, either."

"Thinking about it," Lynda added, "I see the
resemblance."

Lynda's words warmed Tessa's heart.

Her expression serious, Lynda grasped
Tessa's hands. "I know that Ethan told you
about his gambling, but—"

Tessa held up her hand. "I was wrong about
your son. I've been wrong about a lot of things,
and I intend to make things right the instant
I see him."

"Good." Lynda nodded.

Tessa had driven her father to the E.R. in Albuquerque while Ethan stayed behind to unload the horses, drive Kevin's truck and trailer
to the sheriff's office and give a statement.

The E.R. doctor came out, calling for Tessa. Lynda came with her.

"Dr. Adams's X-rays look good. We'd like to keep him here overnight just for observation."

Tessa knew it was the safe route, but there was still an uneasy tension in her gut. After Doc was settled into a private room, they were allowed to see him.

Tessa grabbed her father's hand.

He smiled at her. "The one thing I heard as I slipped into unconsciousness was you calling me 'Dad.' That word gave me the strength to hold on."

"When I drove up to the clinic and saw your truck, I thought, 'Dad's here.' It stopped me, because it felt so natural, as if I had the right.

"I know I told you I'm sorry for acting so childishly, but I want us to start again. I want to find out what it's like to have a father, one I can admire and talk shop with."

"I'd like that. I want to get to know you and find out what it's like to have a daughter. A talented, beautiful daughter."

Wiping away the tears on her cheeks, she smiled. "I'd like that, too."

Doc looked over Tessa's shoulder and smiled at Lynda. "Can you believe what a wonderful blessing has come into my life?"

Coming to his side, Lynda nodded. "It's a surprise, but I can't think of anyone I'd rejoice more for. You, Vince, deserve it."

The door opened and Ethan appeared in the room. Without waiting, Tessa threw herself into his arms.

"I was so wrong about you, Ethan." She looked up into his face. "Please forgive me for acting like a childish idiot."

Ethan scooped her up into his arms and kissed her. He rested his forehead against hers. "You had your reasons." He set her down.

"Thank you for making excuses for me, but I was painting you with the brush I used for the man I thought was my father.

"But when Kevin complained that you ruined William, all I could think was how wrong I'd been. The light went off in my head." She wrapped her arms around his waist and hugged.

"Does this mean that you think there might be a future for us?"

Her head jerked back and she looked at him. "What?" Hope filled her heart.

Doc sat up straighter, looking at them. "Girl, let the man ask you the question."

Lynda grinned at Ethan and her.

Ethan got down on one knee, so that he was looking straight into her eyes. "Tessa, I love you. I've never been so sure about anything in my life. Because of you, I had to face the ghosts of my past and now feel free and filled with hope. I want you to be my wife. Will you marry me?"

Tessa stared at Ethan.

"Tessa," her father said, "if you want my two cents, I'd say you need to accept it. Don't let this opportunity pass you by."

Tessa turned back to Ethan. "Yes, Ethan, I'll marry you."

He stood, scooped her up into his arms and kissed her. The door suddenly opened and Ethan's family poured in.

"We're getting married," Ethan told them.

"About time," Beth answered, just before Ethan and Tessa were swallowed up in a group hug.

"I knew you weren't as dumb as you looked," Zach teased his brother. Zach got an elbow from his wife for his efforts. "I mean my condolences, Tessa."

Sophie glared at her husband. "Don't pay attention to him."

Tessa looked up into Ethan's face. "Don't worry. I know a good thing when I see it." She grabbed Ethan's hand with both of hers. "And I don't plan on letting go."

Epilogue

Tessa looked out the large, plate-glass window of Beth's old room in the McClures' house. On the patio, guests gathered to witness their wedding. The past six months had sped by, with Tessa and Ethan deciding where they'd live and how to arrange the logistics of Ethan continuing work on the family ranch and Tessa working with her father in their practice.

They had opted to build their home beyond the main ranch house. Their garage would also have a smaller clinic, where she could see patients here at the ranch. Two days a week she'd stay at the ranch and take patients there and three days she'd be with her father at his clinic.

Tessa still marveled at the man her father

turned out to be. The amazing thing was that Joan came out several times to see her and Doc while he flew back to Kentucky several times. Her parents were coming to know each other again, slowly, and they both wanted to continue to see each other.

Joan came up behind her and asked, "Are you happy, Tessa?"

Tessa turned and embraced her mother. "More than I can explain." She pulled back and looked at her mom. "I have two wonderful parents, a man who is more than I could imagine and his big, wonderful, hugging family.

"And I'm practicing veterinary medicine with my father. I'm so happy, Mom. What more could I want?"

"Nothing." Her mother smiled tentatively. "I've always loved you, Tessa. I failed you and I'm sorry."

Tessa hugged her mother. "Mom, you did the best you could. I am just glad you're my mother. And look how our journey has ended. I'm happy. And I thank you for being there for me."

Joan's trembling fingers pushed a lock of hair off her face. "I love you, Tessa."

The door to the room opened and her father walked in. "It's time, ladies."

Both women wiped the tears from their cheeks and walked out of the room. As Tessa stood in the den of the house holding her father's arm, waiting for the music to begin, she marveled at how God had turned the broken pieces of her life into a wonderful mosaic.

Doc looked down at her. "This is the proudest moment of my life, escorting my daughter down the aisle."

Beaming, Tessa smiled at him. "I'm glad you're here."

The multiple guitars began to play the wedding march.

They stepped out into the beautiful spring day. As she walked down the aisle between the white chairs on the patio, her gaze locked with Ethan's.

Love and joy flooded her soul, and Tessa offered up her thanks to Heaven above, because she knew that only God could've orchestrated this, giving them all—Doc, her mom, Ethan and her—a fresh start.

* * * * *

Dear Reader,

I hope you enjoyed Ethan and Tessa's story. Ethan has appeared in all three novels dealing with the McClures. He is the dependable, likeable older brother who is the salt of the earth. Yet, because he is the stable one, the one who never grabs the spotlight, and is everyone's strength, he stumped me. Surely he couldn't be perfect. Well, the man knew how to hold his secrets, but with a lot of digging, I discovered his buried fears and flaws. Because everyone thought he had it together, he was ignored and not appreciated. The people we think are perfect and have it together, still have feet of clay and need grace.

Of course, Tessa has overcome a lot, but had to learn to forgive those around her who weren't perfect (which is all of us). It was a hard lesson, but after several stumbles, my overachiever finally learned that lesson. As I wrote Tessa, I felt her anger and confusion. Of course, when she finally yielded to God,

He brought her through the storm into a bright new tomorrow.

I pray you enjoyed their journey, found some surprises and saw a few truths.

Leann Harris

Questions for Discussion

1. Ethan's first meeting with Dr. Grant was tense. Do you think he was reasonable in his reaction? Have you been in a similar situation where you reacted before you knew what was happening?

2. What did you think of Tessa's response to Ethan's assumptions?

3. What changed Ethan's attitude toward Tessa?

4. Mary Jensen is back in Ethan's life. What was their relationship before? How has Ethan dealt with that incident?

5. Both Ethan and Tessa are horse people and find a common purpose. Have you had someone in your life that you were only able to relate to by a common interest, then found a real friend?

6. Tessa tries to get Dr. Adams into the present day. Is there someone close to you who

resists modern technology? What did you think of Doc's attitude toward technology?

7. Tessa's mother surprises Tessa by giving her a new car. Was it a surprise when you learned the truth of Doc's and Joan's relationship?

8. Was Tessa's anger justified or over the top? Have you ever been so hurt and mad that you couldn't talk about it?

9. Joan Grant's first love always guided her. What did you think of her solution to her situation of finding herself pregnant? Was she right not to tell Vince?

10. When Tessa sees Ethan in the GA meeting, she rushes out. Did she handle the situation well? Poorly? What do you think she should've done?

11. What did you think of how Ethan handled the situation with Tessa? With William?

12. Ethan kept his secret of gambling and owing money from his parents. Was that a good idea?

13. Ken McClure told his son that he needed to forgive himself, because God already has. What do you think of Ken's advice to Ethan? Has that happened to you? Did it box you in as it did Ethan?

14. Tessa is almost too late to set things right with her parents and Ethan. Do you think she should've "gotten over it" a lot sooner or was she enjoying her pity party?

15. Do you think Doc Adams and Joan Grant (Tessa's parents) are going to get together? Would you like to see that?